A White River

Being a Partial Accounting of the Liner, Rush and Turpin Families of Western North Carolina, Their Free Negro Acquaintances as well as the 16th & 62nd North Carolina Infantry Regiments in the War Between the States.

George Gary Roland

PublishAmerica
Baltimore

© 2004 by George Gary Roland.
All rights reserved. No part of this book may be reproduced, stored in a retrieval system or transmitted in any form or by any means without the prior written permission of the publishers, except by a reviewer who may quote brief passages in a review to be printed in a newspaper, magazine or journal.

First printing

ISBN: 1-4137-5180-6
PUBLISHED BY PUBLISHAMERICA, LLLP
www.publishamerica.com
Baltimore

Printed in the United States of America

For Laurel

The South is a place, everywhere else is just a direction.

—Unknown—

ACKNOWLEDGMENTS

I wish to thank my cousin, Josephine Corbin, for delving into our family's history and sparking my interest in the Civil War. Prior to her investigations, I had assumed most of my predecessors were horse thieves or bootleggers. I'm sure some were, but I came to learn others were people of substance and learning. I also want to thank Shelby Foote for his narrative history of the Civil War, which forever hooked me on our great national conflict.

I am grateful to my friends and colleagues who helped me in pursuing this dream. Computers are anathema to me, and for that reason and a thousand others, I want to thank my wife, Laurel, who believed in me and made that belief manifest by typing the manuscript over and over.

Lastly, I thank Allison Matlock for her editing, as well as the folks at PublishAmerica for bringing the book to fruition.

George Gary Roland

November, 1860

Word had finally reached Doc at his home near Franklin, close upon the Nantahala Range of the Southern Appalachians in Western North Carolina. Friends in Charleston said that the Palmetto State was intent on secession. Speculation was rampant as to the ramifications of such a decision and as to how it would affect adjoining states, not to mention the rest of the South. It was against this uncertain backdrop that the clan gathered one evening on Rush's expansive front porch, basking in the remnants of an unseasonably warm day. Doc led off: "As you all know, a wave of secession is sweeping through the South. Where it will lead and whom it will involve, I do not know. Yet, I believe it will come. North Carolina's role is not certain. It will, I believe, wait to see what reaction is forthcoming from Lincoln and act accordingly. Whatever the outcome, we will all need to search our hearts for what we think is best. No one here will be criticized for their choice; it is a profoundly personal matter."

Silence settled over the group as they considered the manifest implications of two nations.

"Honest men have honest differences," Doc added, "but I do not favor the trend reflected in Washington towards a central bank, protectionist tariffs, and a mercantile class dependent upon and contributing to an omnipresent federal government that will naturally, in turn, favor those same contributors. I cannot imagine that the form of governance we are now inclined towards is the one Jefferson envisioned. The states are paramount, or should be. Right or wrong, it is for them to decide their course. I am given to understand that some ninety percent of Federal revenue comes from tariffs and, further, that over eighty percent of those come from the South. For what? To make improvements and fund projects in the North. That smacks of taxations without benefit. Mark me: this nation—whatever its eventual form—will rue the day we relinquish power to a central government. Slavery is an institution that must cease.

It is, however, a matter for the South to decide how best to shepherd its end. I fear this issue has the potential, mind you the potential only, to tear the fabric of society asunder. I pray it does not, but if Lincoln calls for volunteers from the South to subjugate the South, as I have heard he may, the Rubicon is crossed, and we will have war. God help us, we will have war."

A pallor came over those on that porch that night as if a curtain had been lowered, signaling the end of an act, or, perhaps, an age.

Chapter 1

"Come up, Sadie," G.N. shouted as he urged the mule forward on the rutted logging road that served as access to the Bullard house. "Come up, girl."

"Storm comin' up," Mary observed from her seat beside him on the buckboard. Dr. Rush opted for this conveyance for practical reasons; foremost among them was that payment for his services often took the form of livestock, produce, cured hams, and an occasional jug of moonshine.

A winter storm was coming up, not an unusual occurrence, except that lightning mingled with the falling snow. They both fell silent, knowing the inclement weather would probably strand them a day or two at their destination.

The delivery was somewhat prolonged, yet otherwise uneventful. G.N. had washed and rejoined the expectant father. "Well, Jebidiah, you got it right this time… twin girls."

"I reckon I'm proud. How's Cumi?"

"Exhausted, but fine. Mary's cleaning up—why don't you go on in."

"I reckon I will," he answered as he hitched up and buttoned the gallowses on his worn and faded overalls.

When all was right and calm and everyone had eaten, G.N., Jebidiah, his son Harley, and Mary sat in the cramped smoky room that constituted the remainder of the house. "Care for a horn, Doc?" Jebidiah asked as he passed the jug.

"Don't mind if I do, Jeb. It's cold, I'm tired, and you make some mighty fine shine."

"I'm obliged. You and Miss Mary can sleep in the house. Me and Harley will bed down in the barn. No sense tryin' to make it back in this mess."

"Wouldn't hear of it, Jeb, though I thank you. No, you belong here with Cumi. We'll put the wagon and mule in the barn. Mary can sleep in the buckboard, and I'll rest in the loft."

"Harley," Jeb stated, glad to have some authority reestablished, "put Doc's mule and wagon in the barn. Feed and water Sadie then put blankets and quilts out for 'um. Hop to it, son. Doc's tired."

"Yes, sir," Harley replied as he rose, gathered some bed covers, and strode towards the door. Turning, he fingered the quilts while seemingly addressing the floor. "Paw, what we gonna call them girls?"

Winking at G.N., Jebidiah said, "You think on it, son, and let me know."

Harley brightened, jammed his hat over his head, grinned wide and said, "Yes, sir, yes, sir."

As they bedded down, the storm heightened but ran its course within the hour. Oddly enough, as the clouds broke up, moonlight filtered through the cold January air to illuminate the barn's interior. Slanted silver rays passed between the innumerable cracks in the boards. As much as he hated to tear himself from the warm burrow he had made in the hay, G.N. got up to relieve himself. No sooner had he tunneled back into his nest, extinguished the lantern, and drawn the quilt up around his neck, than he heard Mary's soft, shuffling steps on the loft ladder. Shivering, she stood before him, the pale moonlight silhouetting her through the makeshift gown she wore.

In a voice equal parts trepidation, uncertainty, and desire, she said, "I'm cold."

"Oh, Mary," he whispered, holding out his hand for her.

Snuggling next to him and warming, she murmured, "We *are* such stuff as dreams are made on."

When Dr. G.N. Rush entered Mary Magdalena for the first time early that cold, memorable January morning, he muttered in a barely perceptible sigh, "God of my wants."

"Lord of my needs," Mary whispered in his ear as she received him.

G.N. and Mary, who was now both midwife and clandestine lover, carried on with their duties as before. Knowing that the lights of a house tell their own stories, by mutual consent and subterfuge, they devised a plan to conceal their relationship that would still enable them to be together when home. Upon retiring, both would go to their separate sleeping quarters and light lamps. After a suitable period of time had elapsed, they would extinguish their lights within a half hour of each other. Allowing another thirty minutes to pass, Mary would make her way to George's bed, their ardor smoldering under the enforced curfew. Should anyone call during the night, as often happened, Mary would rise at the knocking, hurry to her room, light a lantern and then answer the door. In this fashion they preserved the appearance of propriety so often violated in actuality, of 1862 Appalachia, all the while reveling in each other's comfort, presence, humor, uniqueness, and sexuality.

Chapter 2

Twelve-year-old Rebecca Rush, Doc's precocious and lone child from his previous, first, and only marriage, clinched her fists, stomped her bare feet, twisted her face into as much rage as a child of her disposition could muster, and said, "You ain't my mama!"

"No," Mary replied, "you 'aren't' my 'mother' and I *ain't*, but I *am* a woman, I *am* here, and I *am* in charge, so you best unscrew that face or your daddy will wear the hide off you when he gets home." Knowing this threat bore no relation to the truth, she added, "And, you know that kind of talk breaks Mary's heart."

This served to deflate Rebecca like letting the air out of an errant balloon, so she adopted another tactic. "But a bath *and* a dress? Please, Mary, not both!"

"Doc say both, we do both. Liners coming over for dinner tonight. Your daddy wants you to be the lady of this house. Now go or *I'll* scrub you. Besides, I see how you look at that Liner boy."

This shattered any rebuttal or defense Rebecca had, so turning her head to hide the blush, she resigned herself to a fate that entailed both bathing and dressing up while making her way to the back porch and the dreaded tub.

Chapter 3

Rebecca's grandfather, George Wilhelm Rush, was a rising star in the staid, hidebound Prussian army. As a graduate both of his country's military and medical schools, he was destined for the upper echelons of command and society. His young wife Gretchen, while of middle class background, yielded to no one in radiance or beauty. Actually, it was these attributes that drew her to the attention of G.W.'s commanding general, Baron Von Emmerich. Forsaking decorum while depending on rank and station, he made improper advances to which G.W. took umbrage and felt he was honor-bound to defend. The confrontation that ensued saw privilege prevail. An "understanding" allowed G.W. to keep his rank while being assigned as an "observer" to the fledgling American military forces. Embarking from Rotterdam aboard the Neptune, G.W. and Gretchen arrived in Philadelphia during a bleak November in 1821. True—at least—to their word, a stipend arrived with regularity from Danzig, enabling the major and his dashing young bride to move in acceptable circles.

In the course of his duties, G.W. ranged over the Northeast, mounted one memorable expedition to the mid-west, and late in '23 made his way south with Gretchen to Charleston, South Carolina, and what would prove to be their new home. Normally suspicious of "Dutchmen," G.W.'s command of English, medical prowess, obvious military skills, and courtly European manners endeared him to those forming the neophyte state militia, and the couple was soon a fixture in Charleston society.

George Nimrod Rush was subsequently conceived in a rowboat floating around Charleston harbor on a lovely spring evening in 1824. Turnagain Bay, a black midwife, delivered him eight months, eight days later. This event held irony that was as yet unrealized, in that the midwife herself was equally pregnant. Turnagain, a free Negro, was the daughter of a slave named Napoleon Too and his owner's wife's sister, who frequented their North Carolina plantation near Newbern. She—the sister—was a woman of large appetites, none of which involved food. Her pregnancy was discovered too far along to risk taking the baby without endangering the mother, so it was decided she would be relegated to a distant relative's house for the term. Having never revealed the identity or ethnicity of the father, the distant dumping ground cousin was somewhat taken aback when a cocoa-colored girl was born. The mother bequeathed the surrogate parents enough money to see the child to puberty and left. The baby was taken to a local slave family, who was given a fraction of the monies intended for her upbringing, and the cousin left, following close upon, if not the footsteps, then surely the example set by the mother.

Knowing only geographically where the baby came from, her adoptive family named her Turnagain Bay after a body of water adjoining Lukens Island, part of the plantation on which her father still labored.

Through intelligence, wile, and judicious use of her considerable womanly charms, Turnagain had secured the necessary funds to purchase her freedom by the age of eighteen. This was in spite of the fact that she was technically not a slave, although the owner of her "parents" had declared her chattel.

Her liaison with a French General in Beauford, South Carolina, resulted in Mary's birth. She was a beautiful baby, a precocious bilingual girl, and striking woman at only age sixteen.

In his ensuing years of practice, Wilhelm Rush and Turnagain Bay collaborated in hundreds of cases and were frequently accompanied by his son and her daughter. In this manner, the two young people grew up and together. The young Rush maintained that he, too, would someday be a doctor, and Mary was equally insistent that her vocation would follow that of her mothers.

Indeed, G.N. did graduate from medical school, Mary became a renowned midwife, and their paths crossed once again. The two worked so effortlessly and well together that he asked her to join him in his practice, and she did. It was just as well, for Mary enjoyed her profession, kept her own counsel as well as her virginity, and knew, knew beyond any modicum of doubt, that God had intended her for G.N. Rush and he for her.

Chapter 4

Gretchen had pleaded for a more "normal" name for their son, but G.W. reasoned that Nimrod would instill character and, further, that after his son also attended medical school and became a physician, folks would call him 'Doc' anyway, so what difference would it make? G.N. eventually married Latrise DuPree, daughter of a low country society scion. Regrettably, however, Latrise cared more for horses, hunting, and other women than either her husband or a place in the acceptable order of things. She did bow to convention long enough to present Dr. Rush with a daughter, Rebecca, on whom he lavished his considerable unexpended affection and attention, which served to spoil her, but not too much.

In what would prove to be a partially successful effort to avoid the scourge of Yellow Fever, Dr. Rush moved his wife, daughter, and mid-wife/assistant to the high country of South Carolina every summer. It was partial because Latrise contracted the fever in '27 and died one month later. This tragedy served as an impetus to move the little clan farther and deeper into the mountains each summer thereafter. The first year, they crossed the Chatuge River into North Georgia, and the year after that they moved on into the Blue Ridge of Western North Carolina.

This hiatus grew from one month to two to three and in the fourth year, became permanent. Employing the logic of a man settled on the outcome, Dr. Rush reasoned that when they got back to Charleston, it would be time to return to the mountains, so why not just stay? Besides, he liked the place, the people, the hunting and fishing, the fact he was the only physician for miles around and, lest anyone forget, he simply liked the mountains.

"Grows on you, in you, and around you," he would say. "Damn place is systemic."

They purchased, then settled on some four hundred and sixty acres fronted by the Little Tennessee River as it flowed north. Doc liked the symmetry of that notion, a southern river flowing north. Such things attracted him.

So here, near a little hamlet called Franklin, was where Rebecca met her neighbor, friend, playmate, and future husband, Levi Liner.

Chapter 5

When he was seventeen, Levi Liner asked Rebecca Rush to marry him. She agreed, G.N. and Levi's parents acceded to the inevitable, and the couple was joined in April of that same year. The following April, when Rebecca was seven months pregnant, she and Levi moved into their own log home on a tract of land adjoining the Liners, which they had given the couple as a wedding present. Dr. Rush had commissioned the construction in lieu of fees from several local men. Its biggest amenity was undoubtedly a rock cistern situated on a hill some one hundred feet from the house. The spring feeding it was known to run even in the driest years and afforded the newlyweds gravity water at the turn of a tap. Rebecca was also delighted with a wide porch, which encompassed three sides of the structure and held not one, but two swings and numerous rocking chairs for company, just like her daddy's. In anticipation or perhaps hopes of a large number of grandkids, Dr. Rush had instructed the carpenters to build an outhouse with two adult seats and an equal number of lower ones for children, an unheard of extravagance in those hills.

When Levi and Rebecca's first born, Leander, was not quite one year old, Mary said she had received word that her mother had died in childbirth. She began making plans to travel to Charleston in order to retrieve the infant. Coincidentally, this occurrence provided Dr. Rush with an opportunity to conclude some pressing and long-overdue legal business in the city, so he too began formulating an itinerary. The extended family was not surprised then when, at a joint dinner two days later, he announced that he and Mary would go to Charleston the next week.

"We will accompany some turkey drovers of my acquaintance as far as Greenville, then entrain for Charleston. Hopefully, we will return within a month"

Although the trip proved to require half again as much time as originally thought, those remaining on the homesteads were able to quell their concerns, being all too familiar with the vagaries of transportation in that day and place. The reunion upon their return was nonetheless a joyous one with the attention naturally focused on the newborn.

"Mother was said to have remarked that he reminded her of Othello," Mary explained. Rebecca nodded in agreement as she held the child and gazed down at him. "She christened him that before dying," Mary intoned as she struggled to continue. "I will honor her wish. This boy child, my brother, will be called Othello." Applause and laughter followed the smiling youngster as he was passed from arm to welcoming arm.

It was thusly done that G.W. Rush and Mary gave birth to, successfully brought back, and introduced their son to his extended family.

Chapter 6

Levi and Rebecca Liner had been married twenty-six years come April, had known each other since childhood, and been in love with one another before they knew what to call it. Their marriage at seventeen had been as natural a progression of events as rhododendron blooming or snow falling. Rebecca not only had a mind of her own, but, unusual for the day, exercised it with Levi's encouragement. Equally out of the ordinary for such a remote mountain family was their access to books—Plutarch, Cicero, Homer, and Shakespeare. Many of the volumes shelved at her father's had been inherited from his father. Much of it they had added themselves, however, balancing a frugal budget to send away for cherished volumes. Leander especially had devoured the various military texts and manuals. Thomas, their second born, had tastes that ran to the classics and biographies. Indeed, the boy's attentions were so drawn to their favorite texts that Levi had withheld them as inducements and rewards for reading less desirable books.

Rebecca fell in love with the Bard early on, reading and rereading to her family night after night. "I am of the belief," she told them during one of their nightly discussions, "that man knows no thought, emotion, or act which Shakespeare has not chronicled."

The family was, for the most part, a self-sufficient unit, relying on the outside world only for salt, gunpowder, an infrequent bolt of cloth, and ingots of pig iron for Levi's small forge. Most of their medicines they gleaned from the woods and meadows around them. Their garden was bountiful and varied. By constructing a door over a nearby cave entrance, they had an ideal year-round storage facility for milk, meats, and any other foodstuffs sustained by moderate temperatures. A spring heading up at the far end of the cave kept a constant humidity, and was an ideal, flowing liquid coolant as it ran through a trough Levi had constructed.

Chapter 7

Othello knew at age seven that Mary sometimes left their room for that of Dr. Rush's. Fortunately, he also knew at age seven that this was not something for public consumption and should not be told. Regardless of the immediate and natural regard he, Mary, and Dr. Rush held for each other, the order in the outside world of coloreds and whites was obvious. Even more instructive was Mary's obsequiousness and reservation around whites in the performance of her duties. Intuitively, Othello came to pattern his behavior after Mary, adopting the onerous, yet necessary subservience and dichotomy of personality which enabled both he and Mary to survive, even prosper, in the two worlds they inhabited. Yet, it did seem to him that there was a place where this enforced duality was not necessary, even unwarranted. This was the time he spent with Leander. Early on, they began to play together until the time came that they were simply associated with each other by both families. They were spoken of in the same breath. Leander and Othello became one word for one person. They grew up together and grew together as they grew up. Fishin', huntin', ridin', workin' one with the other, year after year.

It was in the comfort and confidence of such a relationship that Othello broached the subject to Leander as they sat on the riverbank, fishing.

"Leander, sometimes Mary goes to sleep with Doc."

"Mama says they love one another."

"Ain't supposed to though, are they?"

"No, I don't reckon' so, but Mama says some things can't be helped."

"I hear folks been hung for less."

"They have, so you need to keep this close."

"But *you* know, *Rebecca* knows, probably your daddy knows, too."

"He does. I heard them talkin' 'bout it. But that's 'us.' *They* don't need to know, or there will be trouble."

"I sometimes wonder 'bout me and them' too."

"*They* or *them?*"

"*Them*—Mary and Doc."

"How so?"

"Like I am a part of 'um, not just took on and adopted like folks say."
"Ask em—I got my own ideas 'bout that."
"What?"
"Ask 'em. Then I'll tell you—I promise."
"OK. I will."
"Now hush, so's the fish'll bite."
"You know Old Man Calhoun?"
"The deaf mute?"
"Yea."
"What about him?"
"You couldn't catch a fish if *he* was sittin' here."

Chapter 8

God made green beans for two reasons: first, when cooked up with some fat back or hog jowls, they constitute a dish suitable for His table, and second, their preparation—stringing and breaking—affords His children an opportunity to sit and talk, all the while getting some useful work done. Thus it was that Mary and Othello found themselves on their front porch one summer afternoon. A large pot, strategically placed midway between them, was the receptacle for the end product as the strings and nubs were thrown to the circling, clucking chickens and their noisy cousins, the guineas.

After numerous rehearsals and even more false starts, Othello had resolved to just ask his question as best he could.

"Mary, you and Doc?"

"Yes?"

"Well, you and Doc?"

"Doc and me what, Othello?"

He scrambled for the words. "It ain't just work, is it?"

Mary rested her hands, still clutching beans, on her lap and looked closely at Othello. "Othello, there are a number of things you probably need to know and I guess—how does one know—now is as good time as any to tell you. *But,* but, before I do, you must understand that what I'm about to tell you is so important, so dangerous, that people's lives—mine, Doc's, yours—could depend on you keeping this secret. I don't mean this is some play pretend way. I mean it for real. We could die. Do you understand that?"

"I think I do, yes. I think I do because I think I know what you're going to say."

"OK, go ahead, let's see."

"Well, you and Doc ain't just nurse and doctor. You—he—ya'll love each other like man and wife do."

"Good, go on now."

"Well, I guess that's about it, 'ceptin you're colored, like me, and coloreds and whites ain't supposed to do that."

"Right, and when folks find out, somebody's gonna get hurt, colored for sure, so that's why it's important no one knows."

"But Leander and Rebecca and Levi, I think, know."

"Yes, I imagine they do, but not because anybody told them like I'm telling you. They just figured it out, and they're good people whom we love and who love us, especially Rebecca, cause it's her daddy."

"Yea, I guess so."

"And Othello, there's one more thing, equally important and perhaps even more dangerous. We knew we would have to tell you some day, we just didn't know when."

"You and Doc are my mama and daddy."

Mary couldn't contain her surprise or pleasure at this. "Well, yes, Othello, that's it. How did you know? Is that OK? How do you feel about that? Honey, I'm so sorry we didn't tell you yet. I hope you understand why and can forgive us, we both love you very much."

"I don't reckon that's the kind of thing you can tell a kid, is it?"

Mary laughed at the man-child before him. "No, I don't guess it is."

Othello continued, "As bad as they say it is for a colored and white to love each other, for them to have a young un', and prove it, is worse."

"Yes, my dear Othello, so they say."

"Mary... Mom... I like the way I look."

The beans spilled over the porch as they embraced.

"Yes, my dear, beautiful Othello, so do I, so do I."

"Mother, I loved you before I knew."

And Mary thought she could not hold him any closer.

"Othello," Mary said as she separated and dabbed the tears from her cheeks, "I think we should keep calling each other Mary and Doc and Othello. It's best for all if we do that, and so we don't get confused, let's do it all the time, OK? Mary, Doc, Othello, OK?"

"OK, it's OK. And now it will mean more."

"Yes, Othello, now it will mean more."

She paused, drinking in her son's face. "Doc's gone to take some corn to Mr. Talley at the mill. When he gets home, I'll speak with him about our talk and then you can too. OK?"

"OK."

Doc came back in a couple of hours, waved to Othello doing chores in the barn and hurried up the steps with a story to tell Mary. "Wait," she pleaded, "I have something to tell you first." She unburdened herself and related her heart wrenching conversation with Othello.

"Good, good." Doc said, "I'm glad the boy knows and that he knows what it all means. I'll go talk with him. Damn, that's a load off my mind and gain to my nature. I was tired of us pretending." He walked out to the barn and sat with Othello on some hay bales. He was searching for the right words to begin when Othello simply stood up, walked over, and embraced him. Doc returned the gesture as tears welled up in his eyes. After a moment he held Othello at arms length, marveling at the love made manifest before him. The boy reached out and caught a tear running down his father's cheek with his finger. "Thank you, son." The man clutched the boy now and held him tighter still.

Watching through the open barn door from the house, Mary now ran to join the unfolding drama.

Doc held Othello out again and announced, "I'm sure glad he got your looks *and* your brains." If George Rush was fishing for a compliment—and he frequently did—his observation fell on barren ground, for Mary's acerbic wit had always been a match for his intellect. It was one of the many reasons he loved her. She just smiled and said, "Me too." Doc laughed, Mary laughed, and Othello laughed. It was the first brick of a family's history.

Later that evening—Othello was sleeping in the barn with Doc's beloved bloodhound, Smudge—Mary asked, "Now, what were you so anxious to tell me this afternoon?"

Ignoring her inquiry for the moment, Doc lamented, "You would think a bloodhound could demonstrate some fidelity."

"Hush," Mary instructed. "That old dog loves you both. Now, tell me."

Placated, Doc warmed to the telling of his story from earlier on. "Well, you're gonna love this. I took the corn, intending to have it ground, but couldn't find Rafe. So, I just left it and made to leave, knowing he would tend to it. Well, all of a sudden, I heard such caterwallin' as you've never witnessed on this earth. Screamin' and hollerin' and carryin' on. I ran to the outcry, and there was Rafe and the widow Jenkins *in flagrante delicto.*"

"What! Rafe and Inez Jenkins?"

"Yep. Rafe had been puttin' it to the widow right there in the mill down in that little antechamber under the gear-wheel."

"Oh, my Lord! What happened? Why all the ruckus?"

"Well, it appears in the middle of their poke, Rafe rose up and the spoke of that wheel caught him on the brow and peeled his head back from stem to stern. Looked awful and there was a lot of blood but no real damage done. I got 'um out of there—fortunately no one else was about—sent Inez home, and reattached his scalp. It was like layin' a rug. I sewed him up, then I said to Rafe,

I said, 'Rafe, I can understand *what* you were doin', and I can even understand *why* you were doin' it, but I'll be damned if I can fathom why you did it the *way* you were doin' it. What possessed you to rise you like that?'"

"'Well, Doc,' he's says all sheepish like, 'I like to watch it feed in.'"

Doc broke down in convulsive laughter. 'Feed in!' Oh, God! 'Feed in!'"

Mary could not contain herself either, but suppressed her laughter in order to admonish Doc. "George Rush, I don't know why you find that so amusing. You do the same thing and take twice the pleasure in it. Of course, in your case, it only requires a brief glance."

"Ha!" Doc rejoined, "to fully appreciate the procedure, I would have to remain upright and observant for hours."

Mary smiled, took him in her hands and stroked him to fullness. "You wish."

Chapter 9

Chores done and supper two hours off, Othello and Leander again made for their favorite fishing hole armed with several fresh chicken livers begged off Rebecca as booty from the evening's forthcoming meal. These former internal organs were brought along to tempt Ol' Buster, the legendary catfish who inhabited their river. Inhabited may well be too mild a word, lacking descriptive prowess suitable to convey Buster's dominion over his watercourse. He was a legend in every sense of the word. His accomplishments, size, appetites, wisdom, and stealth were of epic proportions. Buster had eluded man's feeble efforts to catch him for over fifty years, it was said. He feasted on pigs—whole—and measured at least two feet between his milky, prehistoric eyes. His whiskers could feel out opposite ends of a grown man. He bore the scars of bullets, axes, and tusks. He rose from the murky, mythological depths only when it suited his enigmatic nature. Merely to catch sight of him sufficed to elevate a man to near Olympian heights in the estimation of his peers.

"What's a chicken liver to Buster?" Othello inquired as they made their way to the river. "He'll just suck 'um off the hook and be gone, if he even *wants* 'um."

Leander smiled. The eternal, hopeful, delusional outward manifestation of man everlasting who thinks he can fool an animal. "Probably nothing, but it'll give him a taste for *this*." With that pronouncement, Leander pulled a half-rotted rooster out of a sack and held it up for Othello to examine.

"Phew! Lord, that stinks!"

"That's the idea! Skunk or something killed it the other day and I've been saving it for Buster. I think it's about ready."

"If stink's got anything to do with it, it's *been* ready."

"Exactly! Now let's bait them livers and get busy!"

They set the livers on hooks and tossed them into the sinkhole, letting the line play out. Settling back against a log, they stuffed rabbit tobacco into their pipes and puffed contentedly. Othello spoke first. "I talked with Mary."

"And?"

"I'm theirs," he proudly announced.

"I figured."

"Can't tell, though."

"No, no you—we can't. I hear tell folks over in Webster hung a colored fella just cause he stuck around till after dark."

"Yea. Besides, it's simpler this way."

"I am a big believer in simple."

"Me, too."

"I been trying to square this with who we all are—how it makes us related."

"Well, let's see. My mama's daddy, Doc, is your daddy, too. That makes you and mama half-brother and sister."

"What about me and you?"

"Well, I reckon that makes you my… uncle—half-uncle."

Othello took this under advisement. "I've always wanted a half-assed nephew."

They both broke into grins, the precursor of laughter which would echo between them for decades to come. Othello asked of Leander, "Do you think we ought to tell Thomas?"

"Tell him, yes. *When* is the question. I don't think he would fully understand the implication now. He'd let it slip just 'cause it made him happy and he saw nothing wrong with it. Damn thing is, he'd be right. No, let's wait until he's got a little more bark on him. OK?"

"OK." Pointing to the lines, Othello whispered, "Check 'um—I think I saw a twitch!"

Leander pulled them in and examined the bare hooks. "He got 'um! Now let's get him!"

"By the way, how you gonna hook Buster on them things? He'll pick his teeth with 'um."

"I ain't. That's why I brought this." Leander pulled a meat hook, fully three inches long on the barbed side, from his sack. "Put the rooster on this, and this," he said emphatically as he hoisted the hook, "in Buster."

"Worth a try."

They secured the putrid carcass to the hook, tied that off to a rope and secured the other end round a locust sapling on the bank. They tossed the business end of their contraption into the sinkhole and waited. Ten hours of hard chores, begun before daylight, and thirty minutes of laying in the sunshine on a quiet riverbank sufficed to quickly put both anglers to sleep. A short while later, the violent slapping of the sapling against the ground woke them, and they were both instantly aware of what was happening.

"It's him! We've hooked Buster!" Leander exclaimed.

"Get the rope, grab the rope!" Othello hollered. "Pull!"

Both boys braced themselves and pulled on the taut rope. Suddenly, it went slack and they fell back.

"He's off, damn it, he's come off."

"No! He's rising!"

They gazed, stupefied, as the great primordial beast broke the surface. It was big, big as a man, and weighing as much. His slimy, white underside reflected light like a moist pearl. He rolled his massive, gray head over and eyed his new adversaries. Then, gathering himself, he lunged in one direction, thrust his huge tail in another, and dove, taking the sapling, two boys admiration, and his legend—intact—back into the dark recesses of the river.

"Damn," Leander said.

"Damn," Othello echoed.

They gathered their belongings and made for home—a bit more privileged and wiser than they had come.

Chapter 10

Othello did not ride to war with Leander because he had to, nor because Leander asked him to—they were both too proud for that—but because he wanted to. Their respective families had acquiesced, knowing full well that where one went, the other would follow, and, after a fashion, felt better because of it. One could look after the other, as always. It was a real comfort to those remaining behind. *With* Leander is the only way Othello had known since childhood. Lieutenant Liner would never say so, for saying changed it, but Othello's presence made him feel not invincible, for that made him vulnerable, but unafraid of death, which freed a man. They were made whole by each other. They rode, Leander on Horse, Othello on Mule—not only their kind, but also their names. They traveled through Cartoogechaye and Skeenah, places long ago occupied and named by the Cherokee. Turning north, then east, they reached Cowee Gap at dusk and made camp, pleased with the ground covered.

Othello had rocked a rabbit with his lethal left arm, and they both watched it brown as wild juices oozed through the skin and then, subscribing to gravity, fell, igniting the coals again and filling the already verdant air with succulent aromas.

"Othello, I don't know what's in front of us, ceptin' maybe death and dying."

"Most likely."

"Just so's you'd know."

"I do and did."

"Alright then."

"Alright."

"Now listen—come to it and you got to *shoot* a Yankee with that Derringer Doc gave you, and I'll work it out."

"Probably just rock 'um. Simpler."

An unhurried pause ensued such as occurs between men who are comfortable with each other as they considered the real of the words that had passed between them. Othello broke the stillness.

"Now *that* would be interesting."
"What?"
"Me killin' a Yankee."
"Why?"
"Who they gonna pull for, the dead Yankee or the nigger that killed him?"
"Granted, a proper conundrum."

Othello removed the rabbit from the fire and the spit, sitting it aside to cool. "Reckon what our boys will make of you and me?"

"They'll figure I brung you along to serve up to me."

Othello considered this. "Won't say different, simpler that way."

"I'm a big endorser of simple," Leander added.

"Gonna miss these hills."

"Me too."

They rode out at dawn, the mountains royal purple with mist lying in the valleys like a thick white river. The went east through Jackson County, crossing the Tuckaseegee River, and climbed the majestic Balsam Range into Haywood County. One week and one day later, they arrived in Asheville and formed up with other volunteer mountaineers. After several days of hard marching, they reached Icard, in the foothills of the Old North State. There they boarded a half dozen or so rickety stock cars pulled by a wheezing old locomotive and set out for training in Raleigh. Under these less-than-auspicious circumstances, the 16th North Carolina Infantry Regiment began its arduous, bloody, sometimes glorious, and eventual failed journey to Virginia, A.P. Hill's Division, Thomas Jackson's Corps, Robert E. Lee's army, and destiny.

Chapter 11

There is, of course, a delicate balance between who we are as defined by birth and that ascribed to us by everything which follows. Thomas Liner was born into a void of sorts, outlined by age and place. His only sibling, Leander, was six years senior. Thomas made, as dictated by time and circumstances, his own way. This was not a burden nor a blessing, it simply was, and like so many other things of that era, he just dealt with it. He came not only to accept, but also to flourish in his solitude. His aloneness, while not absolute, nevertheless served to become his friend, a constant through which he saw, deciphered, and interacted with the world. Such accompaniment, at first glance, might be construed as permissive or unstructured. It can, however, be very rigorous and demanding, and such was the case with Thomas. He chose to exact the best from himself and his silent part never wavered in honoring that decision. If he was to plow, stalk, sing, or hunt, his rows must be deep and straight, his stealth undetectable, his voice pure, his kills clean.

Leander and Othello, by association and kin, did not neglect or exclude Thomas. It was simply that many of those myriad things sixteen-year-old boys did, ten-year-old boys did not. Many things, hunting and fishing in particular, could be done together and were. Thomas enjoyed these outings, but in truth, his proclivity for solitude and lack of any need for inclusion or verification by his older brother, when coupled with his distrust of adulation, led him early on to a comfortable place where he had rather do things himself, alone. He was not a recluse, actually he enjoyed the company of his family and the strength those bonds yielded, but, usually, he would rather just do it himself, alone. He came to know the forest, the streams, the mountains, and its inhabitants better than either Leander or Othello, who knew these things well. But Thomas knew them better, and everyone recognized that and admired him for it. Leander would always recount how, on a grouse hunt, Thomas had warned he and Othello of a Copperhead they were about to reach over. "Look first," and then he told them, even though they knew, even though they were his seniors, even so, he told them because he loved them, "sometimes you don't get a second chance out here."

Thomas grew up in a family bound by love, yet matured mostly alone, a strong beginning. They all, Levi, Rebecca, Leander, Doc, Mary, and Othello, were comfortable with themselves and each other, a state conducive to lack of pretensions, an individual as well as a collective strength and a quiet certitude about life. Perhaps of equal consequence, this certitude also led to an acceptance of death, insofar as is humanly possible, an ingrained knowledge that life itself is a continuation, as opposed to a beginning. Folks who live in and near and as a part of nature know this. They see the majesty of such an arrangement. It is not an ideal life, and they are not ideal people, but it is one unencumbered by trivial matters. It does not produce trivial people.

Thomas would distill this alchemy of resolve into a decision that led him from plowing to conflict, from farming to war, from something small to something larger and much more complex, from everyday to forever.

So he too left, in the quiet grandeur of an Appalachian night to find his own way, his own place, in this coming war.

Chapter 12

Rebecca ran from the barn where Leander and Thomas frequently slept to the cave where Levi was retrieving a jar of buttermilk.

"Levi, Thomas is gone, too!"

Levi took her hands in his and by way of some comfort told her he wasn't all that surprised—he had expected it.

"You *knew! Levi*, why didn't you tell me?"

"I didn't know, Rebecca, I suspected. The boy's grown, and I saw it in his eyes when Leander would talk of going off."

"Oh, Levi, if something should happen to both of them, I couldn't bear it."

"I know, nor could I, but grown men make their own way. It would have been useless for us to try to stop him."

"God, do you think he went after Leander?"

"No, probably the other way, to Tennessee. He was asking the Turpins 'bout Captain John and the 62nd."

"So you did know! Oh, Levi! *Why* didn't you tell me?"

"Maybe I done wrong, but I knew you would fret and badger Thomas, and it would all be worse. I'm sorry. The boy didn't ask me. All I really knew was that he knew he was a man, too. We sometimes forget that, what with Leander and Othello growing up together. You know by the time Thomas came along, them two were brothers in every sense of the word except blood. They never left Thomas out, but it was natural for them, at their age, to be together. Thomas was left to make his own way, and he did. I should have told him how proud I was of him."

"Levi, you never showed the least bit of favor to either one. Like you say, it was just the way things were with Leander and Othello. And you're right, Thomas never whined or complained, he just went his own way, maybe not as learned in books as Leander, but much more at home in the woods. Oh, Levi, I do love them so."

"We shall hope and pray for their safe return. Perhaps we'll receive a letter from one or both soon. I know nothing can fix this, Rebecca, but we'll persevere."

"We will, we have, and we'll continue to do so."

Chapter 13

After unhitching the mule and shooing her into a barn stall, Levi reached for the currycomb on the shelf where he kept the equine accoutrements. Stuck between the boards above the shelf, he saw the protruding end of a white envelope. As he replaced the comb and reached for it, Levi knew intuitively what it was, and whom it was from, and his heart raced.

"What do we have here?" he queried Sukie as she nuzzled the envelope. He extruded the single sheet of paper, unfolded it, and began to read aloud so Sukie could hear also.

> *Dear Mother and Father,*
> *Please do not think ill of me for going off. I know I've left you with all the chores to do, but you must believe the last thing on earth I would do is hurt you. I will not pretend I know all of why I am going; I only that it is like a movement inside, carrying me along. I do not know why, but I do know I must. I do not crave to kill any man or harm another, but this thing between them and us is bigger than me. Perhaps if they see people like me fight, they will know we mean it and let us be. I pray to God it is so. Mother, I will be as careful as times allow me. I will write when I get where I am going. If you can, please tell me how you are and if you hear from Leander.*
> *Your Loving Son,*
> *Thomas*
>
> *P.S. I took my gold piece and a side of bacon.*

Chapter 14

After eight weeks of training and four more of just sitting around, the 16th North Carolina was ordered to Virginia. The men of Company L had elected Leander as their Lieutenant when they formed, an honor he swore to justify. Arriving at their new station, Leander, his horse, Horse, his now man-servant, and his man-servant's always mule, Mule, reported first to an innocuous aide-de-camp in the battalion headquarters of Major Henry Wise, a whiskey-soaked misnomer. After having met the major, Leander lectured Horse that if this was what was intended to whup the Army of the Potomac, a cease fire was in order, closely followed by terms of surrender.

"Lord help," Leander exclaimed. "The man couldn't lead *you* to water." His men resembled their major in that they were less a cohesive unit than a motley group of brawling, undisciplined boys hell bent on drinking, then fighting—each other.

Leander tried, unsuccessfully, to train the company in the rudiments of marching, firing, tactics, and the role of a company in a regiment: in a battalion and on up to what an army hoped to accomplish in the field. It was useless, made more so by a useless commander who talked loudly of fighting but actually only drank himself into a stupor each day. Leander acknowledged his own shortcomings, having gotten his limited knowledge from his father's library books and manuals, but it made *sense* to him. He could see in his mind's eye why things were done, how they related to one another, strategy, the role of cavalry, artillery, infantry, supply, and the logistics of battle. It all fell into place for him, so much so that he also knew in a conceptual way that the fog of war could change it all in a moment. He nonetheless just wanted to *do* it. It was *why* he was here. Othello cautioned him to tread lightly, saying there was enough to go around and they would get their share soon enough.

"I know, Othello. I may be begging you to take me home in a week, but these boys—and they are boys—are gonna die for nothing more than stupidity and a vainglorious drunk commander."

"I'll give you that."

"These... men—God, if they're going to die, let 'um be *called* men—come from hard, scrabbly farms in the hills. They put down the traces, grabbed a musket, and signed up. Thought fightin' was glorious, figured we could whup the Yanks in a couple of months. Knew, *knew,* anything had to be better than plowing, swattin' gnats, and smellin' a mule fart all day. Most came off land that's worthless—cause it's steeper than a horse's face. None of 'em had a pot to piss in or a window to throw it out of. They can fight, and most can bark a squirrel off a limb at a hundred paces, but Othello, they're gonna *die* 'cause they don't know how to fight as a unit and those guys do."

"Reckon you're right. Now what?"

"I don't know. I just don't know."

Leander's foreboding proved prescient when, a few days later on August 8th and 9th, 1862, at Cedar Mountain, his Company broke and ran from what can only be described as a minor skirmish in the battle. Major Wise, who could barely sit his horse, had issued contradictory and confusing orders. He then cursed the men, labeled them cowards and threatened to "court martial the lot of 'um." This harangue came when they had reassembled after learning two of their number had been wounded, one had been taken prisoner, and one was missing, presumed dead. The major shouted his accusations in a foul smelling diatribe as he staggered up and down the shame-faced line. Leander thought to break the Major's neck, but while considering the consequences of such a rash act, three horsemen came up. They reined in some short distance off, watching and listening as Major Wise finished cussing his men. After striking one especially green recruit, the Major made to do an about face and fell into the side of a sorrel horse ridden by the lead member of the group, all of whom had now walked their animals up to the line formed by the disgraced Company. Dirt, dust, and sweat combined to obscure any notation of rank among the group, although Leander thought he detected braid on one sleeve hinting at a field officer. The rider, into whom Major Wise had careened, wore a nondescript cadet jacket and tattered kepi hat pulled low over his eyes. Nevertheless, Leander sensed a stillness and malignancy in the air akin to that when lightning is about. Indeed, as the rider reared his head and Leander saw the cold gray intensity of those eyes, he knew who it was, and the hair on the back of his neck literally stood up.

"Major," the rider intoned, "I seldom involve myself in malfeasance at this level, but reports reaching me of your despicable behavior compelled me to act. I was not misinformed. You, sir, are a disgrace to that uniform, and this army and an abomination in the eyes of God Almighty. When sober, you will be tried by court martial and hanged. I will not have such men in my command."

Scanning the group, the penetrating gaze settled on Leander. "Lieutenant, what is your name?" Stepping forward and saluting, Leander replied in a quavering voice.

"Liner, sir."

"It's Captain Liner now, and you are second in command of this regiment. Captain Love, of your 25th, will assume Major Wise's office and his rank. Carry on." Before Leander could reply or salute again, Wise was placed under arrest and the group turned to go.

"God in heaven," Leander muttered as he bent over clutching his knees, gasping for air, "I've just been promoted by Stonewall Jackson."

Letters Home

August 27, 1862

Dear Family,
   I am well and uninjured, though I regret to report that Molly was shot from under me in yesterday's battle. She was all a cavalryman could ask of a horse, and I will miss her. I wish I could say the same of our cavalry, for in every encounter with the enemy, we are bested. The troops under their General Stuart have a natural affinity for their work and take to their operations with aplomb. We are constantly grappling with an enemy who seems to know our every move while we can decipher none of his. They scout and screen as cavalry should while we are employed as nothing more than mounted infantry.
   Nevertheless, they underestimate us and our resolve, and they will feel our wrath and power when Mr. Lincoln finds someone who can really lead this army and instill pride in its members. They fight for I don't know what, but to see their sorry state when captured, I do not see how they can last much longer. You would think we do battle with spectral demons. The men who fall into our hands are filthy, diseased, undernourished, seldom shod and poorly equipped. Yet they possess a fire sorely lacking in our troops and I fear we will have to kill them all to effect a victory.
   My love to everyone. I hope to be remounted tomorrow, for we make our way back to Bull Run.

   Your loving son,
   Jonathan

Chapter 15

In a decision both symbolic and practical, Thomas walked northwest intending to find the 62nd North Carolina somewhere near Knoxville. The 62nd was made up primarily of men and officers from Haywood county in Western North Carolina. One of these, Captain John Turpin, was an old family friend whom Thomas figured would allow him to join. The provisions Thomas carried, though meager, were adequate for a young man raised in the mountains and used to subsisting off the land. Indeed, Thomas, Leander, and their father would collectively and individually go off on week-long hunting and fishing trips carrying nothing but parched corn, a hook, some line, and whatever gun was available. Actually, having both a ground cover, a blanket, and shotgun made Thomas feel positively encumbered with luxuries. He made decent time, fortunate to hitch rides on wagons driven by various farmers and teamsters.

Stopping for the night in an area called Aquone, he started a campfire beside some fast- running water that's noise and velocity belied the term creek. Thomas felt at peace here, a part of the seamless nature of nature. Within a half hour, he had several brook trouts on green sticks hung over a low flame. He drank freely and deeply from a spring, which headed up only a few feet away.

The unmistakable metallic click of a striker being drawn back froze him, too far away from his gun, the space immediately around him too open to run. He swore against his own carelessness and resigned himself to the worst.

"What business have you here?" a low voice growled, followed by the prolonged expectoration of tobacco juice.

"Passin' through," Thomas said, his voice rising an octave. "Didn't know anybody had a call on this land."

"Nobody does, Cuz," the guttural voice said. "Just checkin'." Thomas rose and turned as the biggest man he'd ever seen shouldered his rifle and strode towards him.

"Traylor Crockett," the behemoth said as he extended a meaty paw that engulfed Thomas's. "You always talk like that?"

Extending his hand in return, he croaked, "Thomas Liner. Just when I get excited. Got a bullet lodged in there," he said as he pointed to his throat and his register returned to normal. "Hunting accident. I reckon I've heard of you. Near legend in these parts."

"People talk."

"You eat yet?"

"Dozen squirrels, but them trout smell good."

"Have at it."

"Obliged, but I'll go you one better." He led Thomas to a shallow portion of what he said was called Forney Creek and showed him a rock structure in the middle shaped like a V, all of which protruded about six inches above the water line, the apex facing upstream. "Built it last week. Reckon they're used to it by now." Who "they" were, Thomas didn't know, but he figured he was about to find out. Crockett directed Thomas to the downstream open end of the structure, planted himself beside him, and both began walking upstream. Crockett loosed a stream of dark juice into the cold water. For a moment, Thomas feared he was partnered with a very, very large madman. But just as he was considering a possible escape route, he began to see them—trout. First singly, then others, then dozens, trying to escape from the men's splashing feet, swimming right into a smaller and smaller confine. By the time Thomas and Crockett reached the closed end, they had only to reach down and scoop fish after squirming fish out of the roiling water and throw them onto the bank. Many flopped themselves back into the stream, but two more soon took their place on the mossy incline. "Cherokee figured that out," Crockett drawled as they harvested their bounty.

After watching in amazement and admiration as Crockett consumed over 30 additional fish, Thomas was rehearsing the best way to beg some tobacco off the leviathan when Traylor bit the end off a plug and thrust the remainder towards him.

"Obliged."

"Ain't nothin' in this world free."

"Meaning?"

"Where you headed?"

"Tennessee."

"For to fight?"

"Yes."

"I fancy me a scrap or two, things beginning to take on a sameness round here."

"Well," Thomas mused, "if Mohammed can't come to the mountain, he might as well bring the mountain with him."

"Say what, Cuz?"

"Nothin', just a sorta joke. I would be honored if we could travel together."

"Done," the big man said as he swallowed his tobacco and made to sleep. He could not help but notice Thomas's incredulity as he ingested the tobacco.

"Keeps the worms down, Cuz, keeps the worms down."

Chapter 16

Captain Liner, resplendent in his new uniform—which miraculously appeared at his tent that morning with the "general's compliments," the courier had said—called his men together and addressed them.

"Gentlemen, I did not ask for this job, but I got it. Having it, I am going to do it the best way I know how. You have seen what happens when men go into battle unprepared. Therefore, we are going to prepare. We are going to train and march and march and train until you drop. Cuss me, but not each other. We may die in the months and battles to come, but it will not be because we broke and ran. It will not be because we lost our courage or our heads. Any man found drunk will be bucked and tied. Any man found fighting with any other man will be horse whipped. Any man found disobeying a lawful order will be court martialed. We are here to kill the enemy and kill him we will. Retire. We sound roll at 4 a.m. Dismissed."

"Yes, it was harsh," he volunteered to Othello as they entered their tent, anticipating his friend's observation.

"Jus about right, I reckon."

"We have so much to do and so little time to do it in, Othello"

"Said it was 'bout right."

"Yes, yes you did. Thank you."

"It was, and you're welcome. Now rest, while I rustle us up some supper."

For the first time in over two months, Leander felt both comfortable and entitled enough to join his fellow officers around the campfire at day's end. This gathering served many different purposes, not the least of which was simply to share stories, shoot the bull, and pass the jug. It was not an uncommon occurrence that the ensuing stories reflected a shared loosening of credibility.

"Captain, join us," Colonel McElroy shouted as he waved Leander to an upturned bucket near him. "These kind men were just saying how impressed they were with the work we've done training the 16th." Nods and grunts of affirmation greeted this observation.

Genuinely humbled, Leander responded, "Obliged, Gentlemen. We well may get whupped someday, but we will not break again."

"Bravo, Captain, well said and fairly done," the Colonel exclaimed as he pounded Leander on the back. "Have a pull on this elixir."

"I thank you and am sorely in need of it."

The Colonel swung his gaze over the circle, settling on Lieutenant Cabe of the 130th North Carolina.

"Lieutenant, regale us, if you will, with the story of your wife's hat." Chortles, guffaws and much slapping of knees ensued from those familiar with the tale.

"I think most everyone has heard that story, Colonel. I would not wish to bore my comrades-in-arms."

"Nonsense, Lieutenant. Some have, most have not. Proceed!"

"Yes, sir," and the Lieutenant paused. "Well, it was my custom, when home, on each Saturday morning to join friends in a field beyond our little town for some target practice. I would be remiss if I failed to mention that a jug, much like this one, accompanied these activities. On one such morning, as I was cleaning my weapons and preparing to leave, my wife of only two weeks, Kay, a lovely and fiery redhead, asked me to stop off at the milliner's on my return and pick up some material for a hat she was making. I then inquired of my wife as to why I would possibly want to condescend to so lowly a chore. "Well," she responded, the sparks fairly leaping from her hazel eyes, "no particular reason, but if you don't, you'll never see me naked again."

"Now, gentlemen," the Lieutenant went on, warming to his task, "I was raised to and do still believe that there are what may be called 'defining moments' in any relationship, especially that between a husband and wife. These times tend to set the nature of interaction between spouses forever. I further hold that if a man does not draw a line in the sand, as it were, he loses dominion over his house." More pronounced murmurs of agreement went around the gathering close upon the well-traveled jug. "With that in mind, I rose from the table where I was seated, holstered my two pistols, looked my bride square in the eye and said, "'Calico all right with you, dear?'"

A roar of delight issued from the combat-hardened veterans as they passed the jug round for the penultimate time, their individual and collective thoughts turning to family and loved ones left behind. Rising unsteadily to his feet, the Colonel called for cups. They all stood.

"Gentlemen, I trust that a most merciful God will, in his infinite wisdom, continue to shower his blessings upon us. A toast then: 'To our cause, our country, and our commanding General!'"

In unison, cups raised, the group responded with unbridled emotion, *"TO OUR CAUSE, OUR COUNTRY, AND OUR COMMANDING GENERAL."* A still silence followed as each man gazed into the fire, lost within his own thoughts, beliefs, and fears.

"It is gratifying indeed to be spoken of in such affectionate terms by those under one's command."

As the great, gray charger made its way into the fading circle of light cast by the fire's embers, the group could not help but gawk at its rider. Regaining some semblance of composure, the Colonel came to attention, saluted, and invited the general to join them. "I thank you, gentlemen, but no, I seek your General Hill yonder. Rest easy men, for we have a day's work before us. General Burnside's army is showing signs of movement. I bid you goodnight."

The entourage moved off, following the great gray. Those remaining, most slack jawed, all awed, kept within themselves, knowing the import of this moment. None had ever before, and most would never again, see Robert E. Lee.

Chapter 17

There arose out of the American Civil War many terrible, sad, and unnecessary things. Perhaps most reprehensible were those men who chose neither side, not out of a sense of loyalty to something higher or conscience, indeed lack of conscience seemed to be an essential part of their dark make-up. They shrank from facing any foe on the field of battle, instead lurking in the shadows, falling on the weak, the old, the frail, the women, and the children left behind. They were akin to the grinning, sordid, cowardly jackal, except they were men and chose their way. They had no allegiance, no thought bounded by decency, no reason, no center. Depredation and hatred of all things living coursed through their veins like a fetid fluid.

Such a creature was Tobias Sweeney. His face carried rotting teeth and the malignant visage of a mythical monster with one milky eye, the other falling victim to infection exacerbated by plain old filth and lack of hygiene. His father—if he was such (these matters were always in doubt in the Sweeney household)—was himself the product of an incestuous coupling between his older sister and their father, and he was noncommittal when Tobias murdered an offending brother by stabbing him to death as he slept. On the one hand, Dad reasoned, that was one less mouth to feed, but on the other, he now had a dead worker who had labored well when sober.

"What's done is done. Haul him off and dump him."

Thus Tobias rose a rung in the Sweeney hierarchy. A little later, he would also do-in his erstwhile father with a wood maul, and now the pickings were ripe in the backwoods of East Tennessee. Many were the homes of men absent—gone off to fight, most for the North, some for the South. Tobias ranged far and wide, killing and raping and burning while avoiding the little and ineffectual law sent out to catch him.

Presently, he had just commandeered a wagon by shooting the mules that pulled it and gutting the man that drove them. He had it in mind to bugger the ten-year-old boy and rape his mother but debated the order of things. He settled on the boy, then tied the mother to a wagon wheel and cut her eyelids off, thinking she would have to watch. He had torn and cut the frightened boy's clothes off, knocked him to the ground, swabbed his tiny white ass with axle grease, and was sliding a gallous off one shoulder when Traylor Crockett walked through the laurel behind the wagon. Tobias, never fleet of mind, was struck by the sheer size of the man striding towards him. He was more mindful, however, even mesmerized, by the rage on the man's face as he moved closer and closer. He was, oddly enough, even partially aware of a second, smaller man emerging from the woods, now kneeling and tending to the woman.

"You can have 'um," Tobias pleaded. "Go first—I ain't proud." This may well have been Tobias's last full memory before hell closed around him. Crockett lay one huge paw on Tobias's filthy shirt collar, one on his sagging overalls, and hoisted him over his head, turning and throwing the repugnancy across the road, hard against a red oak, breaking his back. Next, Traylor placed one enormous boot on Tobias's neck, grabbed his bloody, greasy hand, twisted while pulling it, and tore the shoulder out of its socket. He then repeated this process on the other side. With the man unable to move in any fashion, Traylor took his hunting knife and sliced him deep across the lower abdomen, exposing the viscera.

Sheathing his knife, he turned to Thomas, and by way of explanation said, "Fella's Tobias Sweeney. Nuff said." They harnessed their horses to the wagon and made for the nearest settlement, carrying the whimpering boy and his unblinking mother with them. The traumatized boy and his mutilated mother were placed with relatives. Thomas and Traylor turned northwest and headed for Knoxville.

"What's bothering you, boy?"

"I know he had it coming, but what you did to that fella was pretty rough."

"My daddy calls it retribution, ceptin' he would have cut off the offendin' dick, too."

"I've just never seen anything like that before."

"Gonna see a lot worse where we're going."

"God."

"We'll need him, too."

* * *

Country folk have a saying: "A hog'll eat anything." It was with this old shibboleth in mind that Traylor Crockett left Tobias Sweeney alive and immobile.

Chapter 18

Knoxville left Thomas staring and drop-jawed. He had never seen so many buildings, so many people, so many goings on. Traylor motioned him into a hotel bar. All eyes turned as the huge man walked in, darkening the doorway.

"Mr. Crockett, how good to see you again." The speaker was an officious, wormy little fellow who kept wringing his hands while looking up at Traylor.

"Howdy," Traylor responded, not even bothering to look down. "Good to be back."

"Would you like a table?"

"Yeah," Traylor said, pointing in the corner at one occupied by three men. "That one will do." The occupants scrambled to an adjacent table. "Bottle of whiskey and a pitcher of beer," Traylor ordered.

"Certainly, Mr. Crockett, right away."

"They know you here?" Thomas asked, underlining the obvious.

"I've come here a time or two."

When the waiter brought the order, the wormy fellow accompanied him to ensure everything was okay.

"Now what we need here," Traylor said, addressing the wormy one, "is a poke for this boy, cause we're fixin' to join up with the 62nd North Carolina, and no man ought to go to war without having a poke first."

With that pronouncement, the small hands began to rub each other at a frantic pace.

"Of course, Mr. Crockett. Ahhh, what exactly did you have in mind?"

"The best. What's that worth?"

"Ahhh, that would be Lucy, Mr. Crockett, and that would be three dollars."

Lost in his own remembered revelry a moment, Traylor sighed, "Ahhh, Lucy, yes, Lucy. Done. Take him up."

"Traylor, I don't know…" Thomas blurted as he half rose. "You reckon this is all right? I ain't got but one gold piece to my name."

"Poke's on me, boy. Enjoy yourself."

Thomas reluctantly accompanied the vile little man upstairs. Traylor settled back, enjoying his drink as various men and some ladies slowly migrated toward his table out of curiosity and interest in the great anomaly sitting there.

An hour or so later, Traylor saw Thomas slowly descending the stairs, chin on his chest, hat in hand as he shuffled over to the table. Thinking to interpret the situation so as to make the boy feel better about himself, Traylor sized him up and spoke. "No harm in that the first time, boy, no harm."

"Ahhh—well no, it ain't like that, Mr. Crockett. She wants me to come back, and I didn't want to make you wait."

"What boy? Come back!"

"Yes, sir. Now I'm the first to admit that startin' off, I wasn't much account. As a matter of fact," he leaned over and whispered, "actually, I sorta lost control when she just touched me." Standing up and brightening considerably, he went on. "But then, the next three or four times, I begun to get the hang of it. Miss Lucy says I got lots of raw potential, Mr. Crockett, and she wants me to come back, free."

"Free! Good God Almighty, boy. If you don't beat all! Free?"

"Yes, sir."

"Well, hell, boy. Go get it while the gettin's good."

Thomas started to turn, remembered, and in a hushed tone said, "Ah, Mr. Crockett, Lucy said to say hello."

"Hello to Lucy, boy. Now go!"

Leaning back in his chair, Traylor laughed heartily and slapped the table so that the glasses jumped clean off. He motioned the little man over and boomed out, "Worm! Tell 'um I'll be needin' a room. Looks like I'm gonna be here a while. And bring me a dozen ears of sweet corn, a plate of fried taters, two steaks, a loaf of bread and some butter, and another pitcher of beer.

"Free," he mumbled to himself. "If that don't beat a hen a-layin'."

Chapter 19

Thomas and Traylor finally caught up with the 62nd at a town called Zollicoffer. After several inquiries, they were directed towards a small cluster of three tents said to house Captain Turpin. A posted sentry stopped them and asked their business.

"I am here to see Captain Turpin," Thomas responded, "after a long and tiring journey." The sentry eyed Traylor warily but plucked up the requisite courage to inquire after names.

"Tell him Thomas Liner is here with a friend." From inside the middle tent an exclamation arose.

"Thomas, Thomas—is that you?" The tent flap was thrown back and a young officer sporting a black mane and beard stepped out.

"It's me, sir, and I'm glad to see you at last!"

Grasping Thomas's hand, the Captain shook it hardily and said, "Well, Thomas, what an unexpected pleasure. It's good to see you, too!"

Thomas stepped aside, and gesturing towards the imposing figure behind him, said, "Captain, this is my friend, Traylor Crockett."

"*The* Traylor Crockett, I presume! Lord knows, they couldn't make two like you. Tales of your prowess precede you, Mr. Crockett, welcome."

"I'm obliged, Captain."

"Well, Thomas, what on earth brings you to this God forsaken acreage?"

"We've come to join up, Captain."

"Well done! We can use men of your obvious caliber. Come in, gentlemen, and take respite from the travails of your journey." Turpin instructed the sentry to fetch both some rations and the adjutant. "Sit, please, and tell me of your travels. But first, Thomas, how is your family?"

"Leander joined up with the 16th, and Mom and Dad are fine, or were, when I lit out—ahh—left."

"I sense they were not party to your decision, Thomas."

"No, sir, I just did it."

"Well, we shall write them straight away and allay any fears they might harbor as to your well-being."

"Yes, sir."

"Mr. Crockett, your skills are legendary. Might I be so bold as to inquire whether or not you would consent to serve as scout for the 62nd?"

"I would, Captain. Suit me finer than frog hair."

"Excellent! Now, Thomas, your formal training is woefully inadequate. I know you know the woods and can shoot, but this is another animal altogether. My courier suffered a broken leg last week and is not much use to me as he is. I think, in the interim, that position would serve us both if you assumed it."

"I would be honored, sir."

"Excellent. Now I see making their way here our adjutant who will induct you both and the sentry carrying rations. Both of you come back this evening, and we'll acquaint you with our situation."

Thomas, much more so than Traylor, was crestfallen at his induction into the Army of the Confederate States of America. Not so much the actual induction—that swelled him with pride at obtaining legitimacy to do what he had so long sought. No, it was what followed, or, to be more precise, what did not follow. After the formalities, performed in a perfunctory manner by the blasé adjutant, Thomas had waited, somewhat dumbfounded, for issuance of uniform, arms, and ammunition. Having gone nearly halfway back to his tent and other more pressing matters, the adjutant turned, and seeing Thomas' perplexed look, shouted to him, "That's all, son. We don't have any clothes, guns, or bullets to give. What you brought, you've got, and it's a lot more than some have." Embarrassed, Thomas looked around to see if anyone was watching, thrust his hands into his vest pockets, and walked towards a smiling Traylor.

"Don't fret, natural mistake."

"I just figured...."

"I know, don't fret, we'll do fine." They ate the meager rations afforded them, sought out a campsite, a search made much easier by Traylor's presence, and slumped to the ground for some much-needed rest. Tired as he was, the dutiful Private Liner availed himself of this opportunity to write his mother. A little later, as exhaustion overtook him, Thomas glanced over at the recumbent mass of his friend and thought: *It sure is handy to have your own mountain with you.*

At dusk, Thomas and Traylor roused themselves from a dead sleep, took a quick plunge in the nearby creek, and made their way back to Captain

Turpin's tent.

"Gentlemen, come in! I trust you both are now officially soldiers?"

"We are, Captain." Thomas responded. "Ah, should we salute or something?"

Laughing, Turpin saluted them instead. "Not necessary, but the practice will do us both good." Traylor and Thomas drew themselves to a kind of attention; Traylor bent over out of necessity because of the tent's height and returned the salute. "Excellent, now sit, and as the Good Book says, 'let us reason together.' Thomas, how are the good Dr. Rush and Mary?"

"They tend all as far as they can range. I don't know what folks would do without 'um."

"Indeed. They delivered my two beautiful daughters as you know, and have kept me and my dear wife, Blaun, from death's door on more than one occasion."

Thomas turned his hat in his hands before speaking. "Captain, if you don't mind me asking, what do you make of all this?"

"This 'war,' you mean, son?"

"Yes, sir, this war 'tween us and them."

"It is, in essence, a fight to preserve our way of life. Now, many opinions exist about our 'way of life.' The millstone around the neck of the South is, of course, slavery. General Lee has called it a moral, social, and political evil. I concur. Our constitution even forbids the importation of slaves. The issue is how that peculiar institution will cease to exist. The idea is much easier than the implementation. Yes, we have an agrarian economy supported by slavery, but do we dismantle it overnight, thereby jeopardizing the welfare of both the slave and the owner? I have slaves—eleven of them. I did not buy them; I inherited them. Of the eleven, five are either old or newborn. The six that remain are four women and two men. One, Benjamin, is here with me, as he has been since childhood. He has his freedom should he desire it, but he chooses to stay. I can no more conceive of leaving him, than he me. The other man, Jebidiah, remains at home with my wife and daughters. His presence is a constant comfort to me. Two of the four women are married to Jeb and Ben. The others are twelve and fourteen, daughters to Jeb and Ben. I say that to say this—these people are not property to me, they are a part of my life and I theirs. When this is over, regardless of the outcome, I will emancipate them all, but I suspect they will stay, and I will pay them what wages I can over and above their food, clothing, and housing. You cannot paint the South with one broad-brush stroke. We owe our allegiance to our state, not country. We will not have a settlement imposed upon us by Yankees. We are as different as night and day. I do not defend slavery. Can they defend treatment of factory workers, children, and whole families owing their souls to the company store? Traylor, what make you of Negroes?"

"Like every other man, I take 'um one at a time. Some are worthless, some I would trust my life to. All are God's children."

Thomas mulled this over. "Speaking of God's children, don't the Good Book say they are children of Ham, destined to serve?"

"Yes, it does, but, Thomas, as you grow in years and stature, you will come to learn that anyone can prove just about anything using the Bible as authority."

Traylor laughed. "Ain't that so. Take up serpents, it says. Well, *you* take 'em up, I'm gonna let 'em lie, right there on the ground where God put 'em."

"Thomas, I don't pretend to know the answer to these questions, but neither do they. Let us find our own way out of this abyss. All we ask is to be left alone." The three men fell silent. Returning his attention to Traylor, Turpin's countenance reflected his consideration of matters more immediate. "Mr. Crockett, your services are sorely needed here. As you may know, we are here with the primary mission of defending the Cumberland Gap. We have three companies stationed here, guarding the bridges spanning the Holston River and preventing railroad communications from being interrupted. We also have three companies at Carters Depot, two at Limestone, and the rest at Hayesville. Both Colonel Clayton and Lowe, our previous commanders, are ill. Therefore, Major McDowell, a most capable and brave man, now leads us. I wish I could say the same of our Commanding General, Frazer. Rumors are rampant he traffics with the Federals and that money has changed hands. As to the forces arrayed against us, this is where your assistance will prove invaluable. We are facing General DeCourey on the Kentucky side and General Shackleford on the south, or Tennessee side. In reality, with the recent change in command, it is General Burnside's army to our south. They number anywhere from ten to twenty thousand. We have eight hundred and they are poorly equipped. The good news, lest you despair, is that we hold the gap and even if forced to yield, can withdraw our entire command. The battle, it is understood, will open at noon, two days hence, on September 9th. Traylor, I wish you to report to Lieutenant O'Connell at the top of East Mountain and reconnoiter from there. Report back to me in twenty-four hours. I wish, gentlemen, that we could spend more time together in this happy fashion, but duty calls. I bid you good day and Godspeed." Thomas and Traylor took their leave, shook hands outside Captain Turpin's tent and parted, Traylor for East Mountain, Thomas for his gear so as to move adjacent to the Captain.

After reporting to Lieutenant O'Conner, Traylor made his way via a deer trail to a vantage point that enabled him to see virtually the entirety of Burnside's forces. "Damnation," he remarked to himself. "Ain't no shortage of 'um." Within minutes he observed something that aroused an uneasy feeling within him, partially because he could not fathom its meaning and partially because he thought he could. After only two hours at his post, he witnessed the passage of some six flags of truce: three in, three out. This was enough for him to resolve that even though only five hours had elapsed since receiving his orders, the time to report had arrived. Making his way back along the trail, he came across a teamster returning to his wagon on a mule he had just shod.

"I need to borrow your mule to relay a message to Captain Turpin."

"Find your own damn mule, you overgrown lout."

Traylor realized the man was inebriated so he took no offense, just hoisted the babbling driver off the animal, tossed him aside, and rode off, profanities following after him like trailing pipe smoke. He found Captain Turpin together with Thomas, who was studying a manual of arms.

"Captain, I've seen something 'passing strange,' as my daddy use to say, and thought I should report." He told the perplexed officer what he had observed. Retrieving a small notebook from his pocket, Turpin spoke to his new courier while he wrote. "Thomas, take this message to Colonel Lowe's camp and bring his response as soon as possible."

"Yes, sir. Ahh—how should I go?"

"Of course, take that horse there."

"Yes, sir." Thomas mounted the saddled bay and went off.

As they watched Thomas disappear over a rise, Turpin turned to Traylor. "Crockett, I don't like the smell or feel of this."

"You said you don't put much stock in Frazer."

"Perhaps an indiscreet comment by a subordinate officer, but no, he had commanded no respect, either by his actions or presence. Quite frankly, the men liken him to a sissy-boy, not exactly a characterization designed to instill confidence in fighting men."

"No, kinda hard to respond to that in battle."

"Exactly, Mr. Crockett, you have the matter there. Well, let us wait on Thomas's return."

As Thomas reined up before Colonel Lowes's tent, he saw the Colonel reading another message from yet another courier. The dejected look on the martial countenance of the young officer was enough to nurture dejection in

Thomas also. As he dismounted and made his way towards the growing and murmuring group surrounding Lowe, he heard him address the other courier. "Tell General Frazer I am in receipt of his order and will respond accordingly." The first courier saluted, mounted and rode off.

"Well, gentlemen," Lowe fairly spat the words out as he flung his gloves to the ground, "our General Frazer has surrendered."

Thomas needed no formal exchange of communiqués to understand the impact of the announcement, so he hurriedly retraced his steps, mounted, slapped the reins across the horse's lathered skin, and sped off, carrying his somber news back to the 62nd and Captain Turpin. He found the Captain and Traylor seated on cracker boxes enjoying a chew.

"General Frazer has surrendered!"

Contrary to the reaction Thomas had expected, Turpin merely removed his hat, spat, and shook his head from side to side. Thomas and Traylor exchanged glances, both equally puzzled about what to do next. Rousing himself, Turpin looked to the threatening slate-gray sky and murmured to no one in particular, "Surrendered, and not a shot fired. I feared as much."

Traylor could contain his ire no longer. "Captain, are we bound by this?"

"Technically yes, practically no. No, I feel obligated to follow my commander's decision, or rather his capitulation, but you, no, you two do what you will, and I'll cover for you."

"Well, if it's all the same to you, I came here to fight, not quit. I think I'll skedaddle to Virginia where they 'contest these matters,' as my daddy used to say. Thomas, you with me?"

"Absolutely. Let's git and contest."

Turpin's answer was now channeled into something, anything other than giving up. "Take these mounts and grab anything else that suits you. No use handing it to the Yankees. Good luck. Now *go*—I see Federal cavalry approaching."

Chapter 20

Rebecca stood trembling alongside the south facing of their barn where she had been gathering collards that had survived the year's first frost. A letter, hurriedly passed to her by a traveling sutler, shook in concert with her hands. She could not bring herself to look at the envelope and the only clue given by the recently impressed and itinerant postman was, "Letter for y'all." From whom? About what? Oh God, the not knowing was unbearable, but the potential calamity contained in the thin missive was equally debilitating. Torn between wondering and knowing, she stood transfixed. Rounding the barn after slopping the one remaining hog, Levi saw her and then saw her looking through him to somewhere ethereal. The envelope in her hand froze him until he saw it was unopened, raising a brief, tenuous hope.

"Becka, what is it?" His words broke her trance.

"A letter," she said, holding out the soiled parchment. He took it from her, and in one motion, turned it over, reading the address.

"It's a letter from Thomas, Becka, it's from Thomas!" The words lodged in his throat.

"Oh, thank God! Please, I couldn't even look at the address, much less open it. I'm such a coward! Please, read it now."

"Yes, but first, let's go in and sit and enjoy some cider as we do."

"That's a splendid idea. I'm so relieved and yet so ashamed."

"No shame in loving your children, Becka."

"I know, Levi, but they're so brave, risking all for something they believe in and I, I am unable to turn a simple envelope for fear of what it might reveal."

"Shh—speak of it no more. Now, let's read our son's letter."

"Yes, yes, let's do." She took his arm and they made their way to the cabin door.

"Dear Mother and Father," Levi began once again. "That's you and me, Becka," he said with a mischievous twinkle in his eye. He relished any opportunity to lighten his beloved Becka's burdens.

"Oh, Levi, don't be silly! I know who *'they'* are, now read it!"

Clearing his throat, he began anew. *"Dear Mother and Father."* Again he paused. "I am struck by the greeting, Becka." Digressing once again, he was determined to mine every nugget of mirth possible. "Am I not head of this household? Should I not be afforded the respect inherent in that role? Is that too much to ask? I ask you, dear Becka, is that too much to ask?"

"Levi Jordan Liner." Each syllable was slowly articulated. Each word bitten off at its ending. "Read that letter—*now*—word for word, with no editorials, wry observations, commentary, or questions."

> *Dear Mother and Father,*
> *I write to you from Tennessee, where we are in company with Captain Turpin and the 62nd North Carolina. I say "we" because I met and have befriended someone on my way here. You may have heard of him— Traylor Crockett. He is an excellent companion. We have enlisted. Captain Turpin has been most hospitable and inquires after our family. I confess to being somewhat disappointed in the ways of this army. We are underfed, ill equipped, and poorly armed. Nevertheless, I want you to know this is what I longed for and am glad I did it. We have seen no action thus far. Mother, please do not worry about me. I am in good hands. All my love.*
> *Your son,*
> *Thomas Liner, Private CSA*

Man and wife sat in silence, digesting the letter. Levi broke the quiet. "I know of this Crockett fellow—a giant of a man in many ways. Thomas could not have found a better friend."

"Yes, I'm pleased and relieved, I think as much as any mother can be."

"Many mothers and fathers sacrifice as we do, Becka."

"I know, Levi. The idea of sacrifice does not alleviate the anguish caused by it, though."

"For me either, Becka, for me either."

Nodding in confirmation, she rose. "And now, Mr. Levi Liner, because you have fulfilled your obligations here on the home front as instructed, I wish to lift the injunction." With that, she began unbuttoning her dress for reasons not hinted at between them since Thomas had left.

Chapter 21

Shortly after setting out on their Virginia odyssey, Traylor and Thomas passed through a field used by the Federal forces to graze their stock, both horses and cattle. The entire herd was guarded by one indifferent private who merely waved and went back to washing his shirt under a small waterfall. Prominent among the feeding animals was a Percheron draft horse. No sooner had Traylor spotted the animal than it seemed the horse noticed Traylor, as if the largest of both species was paying respect to the other. Altering his course so as to ride by the brute, Traylor had it in mind to nonchalantly tie a rope to the bridle and lead the horse off. As he approached, however, the rapt attention paid him by the enormous equine led him to believe such larceny may not be necessary. Speaking in low, measured tones, he had the animal's full attention. Clicking and calling, he rode by, never looking back. The horse fell in behind him as if he had been doing so for ages. Once out of sight, he dismounted, removed the saddle from his own horse, cinched it up—barely—on the Percheron, and the pair cantered off, Traylor finally astride a mount his equal in stature.

Several hours and some twenty hard miles later, they made camp. Both men were enjoying a chew, spitting the dark brown juice into the campfire, where it hissed and steamed in the coals. It was then Thomas turned inquisitive regarding his big companion.

"Traylor, there's more to you than meets the eye, if such a thing is possible."

"How so?"

"Well, it's sorta hard to decipher. It's just that you seem to keep unfolding depending on the situation."

"Daddy said, 'Never show all your cards.'"

"Now see, that's what I'm talking about. Your daddy, for instance, must have been a natural philosopher; he had something sage to say about anything that came up."

"He was, by nature, a reflective man."

"I'll say. It just don't seem to fit sometimes. You a mountain man legend, yet seemingly wise in the ways of the world."

"Daddy used to say, 'Son, stop all the "roof noise," he called it. 'Listen. Look. Think. Nature can teach all one needs to know.' I did. It does."

"I believe that."

"Wouldn't be here if you didn't."

"Who—me or you?"

"Both."

"Nuff said."

"Nuff said."

They fell into a quiet sleep on earth made warm by the day's sun in mountain air so crisp it broke off with each inhalation.

Although they were unaware of having done so, the Confederate refugees crossed the boundary separating Tennessee and Virginia three days later. As the light faded and a chill began to settle on them, Thomas slowed his horse, allowing Traylor to catch up. As he came alongside, Thomas spoke to him but not at him, keeping his gaze steadily ahead.

"Somebody's following us."

"Have been the last hour," Traylor responded, shifting his considerable weight in the saddle. "Next bend we come to, you take these reins. I'll wait on our friend and call you." Thomas acknowledged by merely nodding. They had only to wait a few minutes before the precipitous mountain trail wound both to the right and over a small rise, affording Traylor an excellent opportunity to dismount, hand his reins to Thomas and secrete himself in a stand of rhododendron. Thomas rode another twenty-five yards to another turn, rounded it, and dismounted himself. He tied the two horses to a small locust tree, drew his revolver from his waistband, and waited.

Back up the trail, Traylor reached over his shoulder and drew the sawed-off shotgun from the holster he kept slung on his back. The double-barreled blunderbuss fit his massive hand like a normal handgun would a lesser mortal. Shortly, he heard a horse snort and knew their stalker was at hand. As the mounted figure, clad in a great coat and slouch hat passed, Traylor stepped from his hiding place onto the trail, leveled the shotgun, and ordered the rider to halt.

"Drop those reins, raise your hands high, and slide off that animal on the left side."

As the rider complied with Traylor's instructions, his horse turned around between the rein dropping and hand raising, so both man and horse now faced Crockett. A Negro nearly Traylor's size looked impassively, first at the shotgun, then at Traylor.

"Now, Boss, do dat left side still apply, or is it switched right, 'cause my left—what was my left—is now my right, and I sho' don't want to git in no argument with that scattergun, or my left and right will be summers in the middle of nothing."

Despite the possible danger of the moment, Traylor smiled to himself, and biting his lip, muttered, "Hell fire, just get down."

"Down I can do, Boss." He slid gracefully from the saddle, landing with both feet together, hands still held high.

Cupping his free hand around his mouth, Traylor yelled, "Thomas, come on!"

"Wondered where the little one was, Boss."

"You can stop that 'Boss' bullshit."

"Whatever you say, Boss."

"Now what did I just tell you?"

"You said to stop that 'Boss' bullshit, Boss. I 'member it like it was yesterday."

"Great God, man, it was five seconds ago and you're still doin' it!"

"Soon as the little one gets here, we'll negotiate, Boss."

"Negotiate my ass! I got the gun, and all you have is two hands in the air."

"Not zackly correct, Boss. In addition, I has my health, a sunny disposition, eternal hope, and a firm belief that the Lord God Almighty is working in the hearts of men to bring us all together, nigger and boss. Occurs to me that it wouldn't hurt none if the Lord dabbled a bit with that huge paw of yours wrapped 'round that trigger, too."

Lowering the gun in exasperation, Traylor sighed, "Heaven help us all."

"Zackly what I was gettin' at, Boss!"

Leading the two horses up the trail, Thomas walked in on the bizarre encounter. He didn't quite know what to make of the huge Negro holding both hands up while the even larger white man merely hung his head and shook it side to side in apparent dejection.

"Howdy, Boss, we been waitin' on you."

"Thomas, see if you can get any sense out of him. I give up."

"Don't *never* give up, Boss. God don't cotton to no quitter."

"See what I mean? *You* talk to him!"

Turning toward Thomas, the dark stranger grinned. "Go ahead, Boss, I's ready, willin', and we see 'bout the able shortly."

Now equally exasperated by the course of the interrogation, Thomas decided to change tactics. "Do you have a gun?"

"Had a little rabbit gun, Boss, but the gun and the rabbit still in South Carolina."

"Then for God's sake, put your hands down."

"See, Boss, I prays for it and it comes to pass. 'Please, Lord,' I says, 'lets me relax my poor, tired arms. Blood done run to my poor, tired feets, and ain't feets nor hands happy.' So I prays and He answers. 'For God's sake,' you says, 'puts your hands down,' and I do, and now feets and hands and everything in between rejoicing. Hallelujah!"

Thomas and Traylor exchanged glances, both wishing they had either just ridden on or been shot from ambush. Thomas shrugged and resolved to try again. "You got a name?"

"Got three of 'um, Boss, all give to me by my daddy, who did love the Lord's creations and named all thirteen of his children after trees."

"Well?" Thomas further inquired.

"Well what, Boss?"

"Well, WHAT-IS-YOUR-NAME?"

"Sycamore Pin Oak, Boss! That's it! Now my brother, up above me and first in line, he called 'Chinkepin Cypress.' One next to me lower on down, he 'Contorted Willow.' Then come 'Horse Chestnut' and 'Gum Cider'...."

"Enough! Quit! Lord, ask him the time and he'll tell you how to build a watch!"

"Right you are, Boss! I'll finish up later on, but don't seem right not to mention the girls. Now they's 'Downy Birch' and 'Evergreen Magnolia' and 'Persian Acacia' and...."

"*Stop* for God's sake, or so help me, I'll shoot you right here!"

"No call for shootin', Boss, I is stopped 'til you say go!"

"Sit down and shut up—just shut up! Traylor, let's hogtie him and stuff a rag in his mouth and ride off, fast."

"Better put the rag in first, or he'll talk us to death while we tie him up."

"No call fer tying or stuffin', Boss. I is sittin' and shuttin', see?" With that declaration, the big man fell to the ground, drew his knees up, wrapped his muscular arms around them, smiled at his captors, and waited. Traylor and Thomas walked off a short distance to confer out of earshot. They shortly agreed on a course of questioning designed to elicit the information necessary to plan a future course of action. Turning back to their recumbent prisoner, Traylor led off the inquiry with a caveat.

"Now listen—ahhh—'Pin Oak,' we're gonna ask you some questions, and we want straight answers. No family trees, just answers, you hear?"

"I does, Boss, question away! Sycamore gonna answer straight."

"Where you from?"

"Six Mile, Boss."

"South Carolina?"

"South Carolina."

"What you doin' here?"

"Sittin', Boss."

"Now, damn it! You know what I mean. How did you come to be here?"

"Shame and humiliation, Boss, shame and humiliation."

"Sycamore, I'm gonna fetch you one upside the head...."

"Truth, Boss, truth!"

"Ah, hell! *Alright*! *What* shame and humiliation?"

"This here, Boss." Turning away while rising to his knees, the big Negro pulled up his ragged, course poplin shirt revealing several festering lashes across his broad, muscular back.

"Damn!" Traylor exclaimed, looking away.

"Boss man give 'um to me 'cause he say I steal. I don't, but he say I do, so dat's dat. Don't make no nevermind. I been whupped before, but dis time, da man make my little chil-ren watch. Shame and humiliation, Boss, shame and humiliation."

Thomas broke the awkward silence. "So...."

"Well, Boss, dat require sum 'splaining. Sycamore been workin' and fist fightin' lo de's ten year. Boss man put me up agin all comers, and Sycamore make a little money, puts it back. Finally, I gets enuf to buy me and my babies. Sycamore's wife die of da consumshun. Day come and da bossman say I steal. I don't, but he say I do, and dat's dat. He say price go up and I gets da strap. Well, Boss, what is a Sycamore gonna do? I gets strapped and just buys my own self. Boss whip me in front of my babies. Shame and humiliation, Boss. So I leaves, and now Sycamore goin' north and work and gets his babies. Buy back my own chil-ren, Boss. Don't seem right, do it?"

"No, it don't. Who was your... 'Boss'?"

"Massa Cooper, Boss."

"Lane Cooper. I heard of the bastard and his wife."

"Lord, Boss, that woman is the devil's handmaiden. No disrespect, Boss, but she in wid Satan."

"Don't doubt it. Ain't even any white folk likes that son of a bitch."

"Sycamore done took all he can take, Boss. Had to git or kill somebody.

Then I hang and Sycamore's children don't got no daddy and no chance."

"God, what a gaum."

"That it is, Boss, surely it is."

"Damn a bunch of slavery!" Traylor shouted. "Damn it and what it's done to my people and my country!"

"Ain't been too agreeable wid my folk either, Boss."

"No, no it hasn't. I sometimes wonder who has been enslaved."

"You talkin' fee-loss-I-fee now, Boss. Maybe boff of us, but I's the one what's got his skin laid open."

"Yes, that's a fact, not an idea."

"Well, now what?" Thomas interjected.

"Damned if I know," Traylor responded. Thomas looked now at Sycamore in a somewhat different light.

"How'd you know we wouldn't just shoot you or send you back?"

"For *sure* I didn't, but I knows you boff enough to know how you thinks and feels." Puzzled now, Thomas exchanged a look with Traylor and continued.

"How you know that?"

"Jus watchin' and listenin', Boss."

"But we just met."

"Not zackly, Boss. Been trailin' you three days now, watchin' and listenin'. Ever now and den, you talks 'bout folks you says is colored, like dis Othello fella an da lady name Mary. You talks bout 'em likes dey real, sure enuf peoples, not just stuff. Sycamore know."

This revelation stunned and embarrassed the two woodsmen. To think anyone could trail them undetected was an affront to their skills as mountain men. The realization that this had happened, that Sycamore could have taken them out at any time of his choosing and further, that he had probably *allowed* them to capture him was, in a word, humbling. As if on cue, they both said, "Well I'll be damned."

Sensing their distress, Sycamore sought to alleviate their suffering. "Don't fret, Boss. Black man born to disappear 'round white folk. Boss, if I could just travel long wid you a while, say I's your nigger, won't nobody know no different, and when you gits where you goin', I just slips off."

"Don't matter to us, but you ought to know where we're going is General Lee's army, to fight Yankees."

"Lord help Sycamore Pin Oak. Yankees or Rebs, what's a nigger to do?"

"I thought you was going north to freedom and get help to buy back your young 'uns?"

"I is, Boss, but it ain't much of a choice, is it? Sumthin' wrong wid a Yankee anyway, ain't it? Just sumthin bout 'um ain't right. Sycamore got a cousin up what be in New Yawk. Say if you think they treat a nigger better, better think again. Say dey won't look you in da eye, like you ain't even der. Say dey won't *call* you a nigger, but shore do treat you like one, like da word worse than da deed."

"Well, Sycamore, we can't fix none of that, but if you want to tag along, you can. If not, we won't tell."

"Believe I go wid what I know, 'stead of what I don't."

"'Better to bear those ills we have than fly to others we know not of.'"

"Zackly, Boss, who say dat?"

"Fella called Shakespeare."

"He a white man?"

"Yes."

"Huh. Smart, too. Maybe Sycamore talk to him some day. See what else he say."

"Maybe, Sycamore, maybe so."

Chapter 22

The unlikely trio made their way into northern Virginia with Thomas feeling as if he had been sandwiched between two gigantic bookends: one white, the other black. He nonetheless admitted—to himself—that he did feel secure riding between the two colossuses, as evidenced by the startled reactions of fellow travelers and those they merely passed enroute. Many initial hostile reactions or potential confrontations melted away when the would-be adversarys sized up their foes. Thomas thought to himself, *It's good to be big.*

From behind, Sycamore's resonate voice called out, "Hit shore is, Boss," finishing Thomas's inner musing. "Now I ain't gonna maintain being big and colored is sumthin' to write home about, but Sycamore reckons hit beats being colored and little. Dat's a double whammy."

Incredulous, Thomas turned in the saddle and looked at Sycamore. "How did you know what I was…?"

"I jus' does, Boss. Comes to Sycamore clear as glass. Can't help it, jus' does."

"Well, I'll be damned. A fella can't even think in private."

"Now, Boss, don't get all worked up. Sycamore 'gree wid you."

"That ain't… I mean it isn't that… I just… oh, the hell with it."

"Dat's a good place for it, yes, sir."

Turning back round, Thomas sighed and spoke. "Sycamore, I don't know about you. It appears there is more to you than meets the eye. Sorta like that big one up there."

"Big is more 'an size, Boss."

"I ain't even gonna try and fathom that. Just watch my back, will ya?"

"Have been for days now, Boss, and I ain't talkin' bout ridin' behind neither."

"No, I didn't think you were. Glad you're back there, Sycamore."

"Ride on, Boss, ride on."

Traylor, inadvertently eavesdropping, laughed to himself and kept going.

From stragglers, camp followers, and some they felt were just plain old deserters, the trio had formulated a pretty good idea of where the army of

Northern Virginia had been and was going. After making camp for the night, they discussed how best to proceed, for it was their consensus that tomorrow would bring them into contact with the storied forces of Robert E. Lee.

"Sycamore, it ain't no mystery what we plan to do. Thomas and me aim to join up with his brother's bunch, the 16th North Carolina. What about you?"

"Hit come to me, Boss, dat da best I can do—Sycamore always strivin' for da best—is stick wid you two, if dat meet wid ya'll's approval. My daddy always said, 'Better to want what you don't have....'"

Traylor chimed in, finishing, "Than to have what you don't want."

"How you know dat, Boss?"

"My daddy used to say the same thing."

"Hum?"

"Hum?"

Chapter 23

Pushing the tent flap aside, Leander looked round and shouted, "Othello!" as he stepped outside.

"Sir?"

"Tell Sergeant Grant I need him and to bring the morning roster."

"Done."

While awaiting the Sergeant Major's arrival, Leander poured over a map furnished him by Major Hensley, General Hill's adjutant. As the heat drove temperatures inside the tent up, Leander opened both flaps in a vain effort to make the interior more comfortable. Moments later, Sergeant Grant arrived clutching the roster book.

"How many fit for duty, Sergeant Major?"

"By company?"

"Total."

"Five hundred forty-six, sir."

Surprised by his quick response, Leander asked, "You know that without looking?"

"It's my job, sir."

"So it is, so it is. Now, from that group, I wish you to select seven of your best men in addition to yourself for a scouting mission. Dangerous, but essential."

"More dangerous than gettin' killed, Captain?"

"No, Sergeant, no more dangerous than that, just additional."

Page by page, Grant carefully drew his finger down the lists of names by companies, mumbling to himself as he did so, keeping a mental tally of those he had chosen. "I have them, sir."

"Excellent. Go round to each company, don't cause a fuss, just gather the men and have them report here."

"Yes, sir." Closing the book, he set off.

Intrigued now, Othello asked, "What's up?"

"It looks like the battle will be joined day after tomorrow. All the pieces are in place, but we don't know exactly where theirs are—hence the scouting party. Apparently General Hill is not too enamored of his cavalry's performance of late. He thinks we may have an opportunity to roll up their left flank—that is if it is not properly anchored. If so, and we can detect it, that information, properly acted upon, could swing the tide of battle once underway. We shall see."

"And who is to lead this party?"

"I am."

"Then there's to be one more."

"No, Othello, you have to stay, my friend. My orders are specific. Eight men—myself and the Sergeant—and two groups of three. We will set out, on foot, immediately, once they arrive. We have a great deal of territory to cover. I should return no later than dark tomorrow. Wish me well."

"If that's the way it has to be, then go with God."

The men selected came to Leander's tent individually and in groups of two or three. They were a hard lot, veterans, sinewy, with bronzed faces and a quiet confidence born of battle and the sure knowledge that it was all a matter of chance anyway.

So as not to draw unnecessary attention to the group, Leander led them a little ways off into a copse of birch trees. "Gentlemen, our task is to scout the flank of the enemy arrayed against us. You know what we face. It is my hope that if we are successful, the odds might favor us for a change. It will be dangerous work, but the information gained could make a real difference in the battle to come. If you don't want to go, don't. Nothing will be said. You were chosen because you are good soldiers—our best. Questions?"

The group was silent, save an occasional cough, spit, or fart. A grizzled veteran of the 16th raised his bandaged hand. "Well, Captain, this ain't no question, but I feel bound to say that if this lot is the best we got, we ain't got a whole lot." Laughter ricocheted through the group, breaking the tension.

"Let's move out. Carry nothing but your weapons and a day's rations."

"Hell, Captain, a day's rations is all we got."

As the group wound its way out of camp, the other soldiers rained insult upon jibe down on their heads.

"Givin' up, are you, Luther?"

"We got a little engagement comin'. Where you goin'?"

"Gonna miss the dance, fellas."

"Come back, Jack—I didn't mean it."

"One hell of a way to get out of owing a fella fifty cents, Duncan."

"We'll let you boys know how it turns out—where do we write?"

The party left, making its way towards the pickets and vedettes set out by the Federals. Leander turned and whispered to Sergeant Grant, "Tell them we wish no engagement—avoid contact." The word was passed down the line, much to the dismay of some of its members.

Hours after darkness had fallen, Leander led his little band up a small rise composed of mine trailings near where he thought should be the end of the Federal line. There was no one there. The left flank of the union line was indeed "in the air." Reversing route, they traveled nearly another mile before they spotted an encampment. Leander's martial blood began to course faster. Marking the necessary information on his map, he quickly sketched two other, simpler copies, divided his men into three groups, and sent them by different routes back to camp. This was, he knew, a calculated risk. While it increased the chances of at least one map making its way to General Hill, it also at the same time escalated the possibility of detection or capture. The map alone would suffice to forewarn a competent opponent, and despite his men's disdain for their foes, he knew them to be a formidable and worthy adversary.

He had assigned Sergeant Grant to lead one group back. He took another and entrusted the last to Corporal Duncan Daylight. Daylight had, at one time, been General Hill's chief scout before being busted for insubordination. Nevertheless, both Leander and Sergeant Major knew the Cherokee to be one hell of a soldier and tracker. Those that served with him spoke with reverence of his skills in the woods. He was, they said, a "spirit mist."

A waning moon lent enough light for cautious travel while cloaking movement to all but the most inquisitive eyes. Proceeding with due diligence, all three groups had made it nearly halfway back when Daylight's squad inadvertently found themselves caught between two Union soldiers from a Rhode Island brigade, one relieving the other from pickett duty.

"Who's there?" the oncoming soldier shouted into the night. "Identify yourself! Ray, is that you? Say something—it's Cecil."

"Cecil, over here!"

Hearing the challenge, Duncan first thought "green kid," then "shushing" his men, he quickly sidestepped the trail they were on, drew his knife, waited, then pounced unheard on the befuddled Ray, severing his throat. Dropping his prey to the ground, he constricted his mouth and made to imitate—not a hard task for one given to mimicking animals his whole life—the distinctive voice that had called out. "Cecil! Here, over here!"

The unwary Cecil, happy to dispel his mounting concern, strove to drive his way through a tangle of brambles towards the welcoming voice. Entering the clearing, he cursed the briars clinging to his shirt and turned to extricate himself from their thorny grasp. The knife entered his back low at the same time that a calloused hand clamped his mouth closed. Not one sound, save a muffled breath, had emerged from either man. The two bodies were dragged a short distance and thrown down an old mine shaft. All signs of a struggle and the copious amount of blood were covered over. This, it was hoped, would lead the Federals to believe, or at least speculate, that the two guards had simply gone AWOL. At any rate, it would, in all likelihood, buy them enough time to make good use of the information gleaned that evening.

Chapter 24

Remarkably, despite their respective routing, all three teams dispatched by Leander arrived in camp within an hour of each other. Leander quickly debriefed each group, marveling at Daylight's exploits and filing them away for further reference. He then retrieved the other maps and made his way to Major Hensley. He repeated his findings to the adjutant, showing him the disposition of Federal forces as he understood them. Pointing to the area encompassed by his reconnaissance, he noted two regimental flags he had seen in their camps. The major seemed particularly interested in this information.

"Yes, we were unaware of their presence, assuming they were still guarding the ford. This can only mean they have all their forces up now and still their flank lies exposed. This will be of vital interest to General Hill. You have done well, Captain."

"My men performed admirably."

"Yes, of course, ya'll stand down now. I will notify you of any decisions reached. Thank you."

"My pleasure, sir." Leander turned and started towards his own tent. Halfway there, he was overcome with a profound tiredness that made him doubt his eventual arrival at his own quarters. It was at this point that Othello stepped out from behind a supply wagon and fell in beside his friend. Leander smiled at this, yet another example of his companion's knowing. He was able to partially allay his exhaustion by placing a hand on Othello's near shoulder, supporting himself the remainder of the way. Eschewing any other gesture or word, Leander fell heavily onto his blanket and was instantly asleep. Othello closed the tent flaps and took up station outside, resolved to allow nothing but nature to wake his ward.

Unfortunately, generals are sometimes construed to be forces of nature, and thus it was a mere four hours later when Othello roused Leander from a deep, dreamless sleep with news that General Hill had ordered a flanking movement involving an entire division.

The logistics of implementing such an order were staggering. In an effort to reduce the process to its simplest elements, Hill had ordered all non-essential personnel, trains, and baggage to the rear. He wanted only soldiers with arms, ammunition, and one day's cooked rations sent forward. Leander's regiment was in the vanguard of the ensuing forced march, setting a withering pace for eighteen odd miles, arriving at 2 a.m. They ate their rations in the cold pre-dawn air without benefit of campfire, their use having been expressly forbidden. After an hours rest, they were placed into line of battle, awaiting enough light to attack the still unsuspecting Federal forces.

It was an unmitigated success. While sustaining relatively few casualties, the triumphant Rebs captured over one thousand prisoners, eighteen cannons, one very angry half-dressed general officer, along with substantial stores, weapons, beef cattle, horses, mules, and several ammunition wagons.

Thus, Othello (recently declared essential personnel) was doubly perplexed when an apparently despondent Leander returned to their makeshift camp near the morning's jumping off-point.

"What's wrong? I thought you would be overjoyed."

"Pleased, yes. Overjoyed is an emotion for novice soldiers or naïve politicians. We have struck them a significant blow, but to hear it described, as I have, by some as 'crippling,' is nonsense. We have struck them one 'crippling blow' after another, and yet they remain ambulatory. I fear, my friend, their resources in men, manufacturing, agricultural, and monies will suffice to overcome any amount of courage, leadership, or military superiority we may have. Pope feeds troops into battle like corn to a grinder. Our garden does not bear. Our resources are fast becoming exhausted. Unless we gain recognition by either France or England, I see no way we can prevail. Thus victories like those we won today are essentially meaningless."

Othello pondered this a moment then declared, "To hell with it then, let's go home."

"I've thought about it, but you know better than most that some things transcend practical considerations. If we are to be vanquished by 'those people,' as General Lee calls them, our honor may well be all we have left to sustain us. In that unpleasant eventuality, we must nurture and preserve that precious commodity with all we have."

"I guess you can't eat it, but nothing else would be palatable without it."

"Well said, old mole. Let us therefore conduct ourselves so that when we recount our 'St. Crispins' day, men will long to have been here also. Meanwhile, these smoked oysters should help us manage."

"Smoked oysters!"

"Case of 'um."
"Damn!"
"Oysters, bullets, and boots. See what I mean?"
"I do! Well, let's eat 'um before somebody declares a truce!"
"An excellent idea, my friend."

Letters Home

I am Hiram Hunt. I hail from Cullowhee, North Carolina. I want to rite down what is goin on and what I think about it. I think a private shud do this so folks can see this hear war like a reglar fella does. I can say this now it is hell. Sleepin in the cold rain, eatin raw corn if you can git hit. Marchin here then thar. Shoddy shoes if you got airy sorry equipmint and poor ol guns. Anyway, the fellas just laff and make jokes and keep on goin and fightin. I think a lot of us come for the thrill thinking we would shoot us a bunch of Yankees and they would quit and go home. Nope. They is here till this thing is done. Some talks about why this thing come about and why it keeps goin on. Hell, us on the line do it just cause of the fella next to you. I don't give a tinkers dam for states rites long as they leave us alone or coloreds neither. I aint got none. I ask what will they do if they was all free today. Don't seem like much would change xcept a idee but maybe that counts two. If they is like me, food and cloths and a place to git in out of weather is at the top of my wants. I figure they is enuf like me to want that two.

I have seed many a fight and many boys die and git hurt. I have seed the livin envee the dead. It don't take no genral to see we is getting the wurst of this. It seams to me we lose even when we win. Like the other day we run over a bunch of green yanks and the stuff they left behind was better than what we got. It is like that over and over. We keep getting stuff from them, not our own, and then fightin over it our own self half our artillree shoots us and the rest don't even go off. They can lob stuff way futher than us and hit what they aim at. Hits right despondent to hunker down and let um shoot at you. Our horses and mules look like they is on thar last leg, if they got fore left. It makes us sorrowful to whup um agin and agin and it don't matter. Somebody said a yank private eats like a reb genral. Now eatin don't win a fight but it shor helps befor and after. I don't know I still git my dander up and I don't like um much. I just wish they would go home and let us be.

Chapter 25

"Captain?"

"Yes, Lieutenant, what is it?"

"Well, begging the Captain's pardon, but some of the other officers asked if I would come talk to you. Truth be told, we drew straws and I lost. I mean won, I guess."

"Then I suggest you do their bidding, Lieutenant. Again, what is it?"

"Well, sir, we was just wondering about your nigger, Othello."

"Wondering what, Lieutenant?"

"Well, sir, is he or ain't he your nigger, cause he shore don't act like one."

"Lieutenant, I assumed this would come up sooner or later, so I want you to listen very carefully to what I say and convey it to the others. When I say convey, Lieutenant, I mean it in the true sense of the word. Not just the words, but the meaning behind them. Is that understood?"

"Yes, sir, I think so."

"Very well then." Leander sat on a stool and motioned the Lieutenant to do the same on an adjacent cracker box. "Lieutenant, I know this war has been portrayed as one about slavery. Well, it is, but that's not all it is. I don't give a tinker's damn about slavery. Owning another human is anathema to me. Others feel, however, we have an obligation to Negroes to nurture them and bring them up to where we are. A load of crap, if you ask me. Where would you be if someone jerked your ass up, stuffed it in a ship, sold you, and set you to work? No, if anything, Othello disproves that bunk. Some think the Bible endorses it. It's been my experience that the Bible can be used, and I mean used, to prove just about anything. What we do know, Lieutenant, is that slavery holds up the economy and therefore the lifeblood of the South. What we also know is that, as we speak, it's legal. Maybe repugnant, but legal. Some of the stories I've been told about workers in the North far surpass in cruelty any slavery I've ever known. I fight because my state asked me to and because I don't want any damn Yankee coming down here and telling me how to live. And, Lieutenant, make no mistake, come they will. Most, I think in the South, just ask to be left alone. Let us solve our own problems, and believe me, slavery is a problem, for the Negro and for us. Left to its own devices, I feel it will die a natural death of its own volition."

Here Leander paused, fingered his sword, and strove for words.

"Nevertheless, to address the specifics of your inquiry, no, Othello is not my nigger. He is a free Negro and further, a free Negro that has been my friend and companion since childhood. You may carry this information to the others, and if anyone, anyone, has any problems with it, they may feel free to come see me about it. Additionally, the men are to address Othello as just that, Othello, not nigger or darkie or boy. Tell them that, Lieutenant, and tell them I mean it."

The Lieutenant stood and began to back out of the tent. "Yes, sir, we didn't mean no disrespect, sir, we all like Othello—think he's a fine Nig—a fine person."

Suppressing a smile, Leander thanked the Lieutenant and also asked him to convey his thanks to the others for their understanding. Othello entered a few moments later and sat down on the box previously occupied by the inquiring Lieutenant.

"Box seems mighty warm, maybe even a little wet."

"I had a visitor."

"Yes, I know. I thank you."

"You'd have done the same for me."

"No, I wouldn't."

"What! Why not?" Leander seemed genuinely perplexed.

"Cause you're a half-assed nephew and just don't have the color for it." The laughter echoing from Captain Liner's tent seemed to reinforce the notion that this was indeed not a typical black-white relationship.

Chapter 26

This knock was different. In fact, it wasn't even a knock, more of an incessant banging on the door with something other than a fist. The accompanying noise—voices, horses—and lights indicated several people, all insistent. George sent Mary straight away to her room and resolved to investigate the ruckus for himself. Throwing open the door, he was confronted by a Federal officer and troops.

"Dr. Rush?"

"I am."

"Captain Anderson. May I come in?"

"Do I have a choice?"

"No, sir."

"Then, please, by all means." Doc spat out the invitation. The Captain entered, removed his hat, and closed the door behind him after posting a sentry outside.

"To what do I owe the pleasure of this visit, Captain?"

"We have it on good authority, Doctor, that you have been harboring Confederate soldiers."

"I fail to see how one can 'harbor' a native in his own country, Captain, but what I have and will continue to do is treat the sick and wounded."

"Nevertheless, it is my task to round up any Confederate soldiers, militia or sympathizers in this district. Towards that end, I will require a list of all those have availed themselves of your services over the last six months."

"Women and children also?"

"Do not be flippant with me, Doctor. I did not ask for this job nor do I want it, but I have it, and I take the responsibility very seriously."

"As I do mine, Captain. I treat the sick and wounded, sir, no matter their allegiance, color, or standing. That practice is no concern of yours or those you represent. Now take your men and go."

"Who else is here?"

"That, too, is none of your concern. I have asked you to leave."

"Better you tell me than have my men find out."

"My mid-wife assistant."

"I cannot force you, Doctor, but be warned, we will be watching you."

"Watch, it is of no consequence."

"We shall see. Now, I wish to submit your medical ethics to a real test. One of my men has a gangrenous infection. Will you see him?"

"I am a doctor. No more need be said."

The Captain called out to the posted sentry, "Private, have Sergeant Reeves brought in." A moment later, three soldiers entered. Two stood on either side of the third, whom they supported as he hobbled.

"Bring him into this room," Rush instructed as he lit a lantern and led the way. "Set him on the end of this table." The soldiers did as they were told and left after being dismissed. The patient grimaced as he moved, trying to find a comfortable upright position.

"What is it?" Rush asked the sweating, ashen-faced boy.

"My leg, Doc. Got a stob stuck in it last week."

"Let's see—I am going to cut your britches open to get at it." As he began to snip the filthy cloth, the noxious smell of festering flesh assailed his nostrils. The Captain, standing nearby, turned away, holding his hand over his nose.

"God Almighty, that stinks." The leg was black to a point several inches above the knee and swollen twice its normal size. A large pocket of pus oozed out of his calf muscle.

"What do you think, Doc?"

"I think you will die unless we remove this leg."

"Oh, hell, Doc, do we have to?"

"Your leg, or your life."

"Well, damn. Cut her off then."

"Captain, I'm going to fetch my assistant. We will use what little anesthesia I have, but we will still require two of your men to hold him. If you have whiskey, give him some. I will be back shortly." He made his way to Mary's room and found her already dressed.

"I heard—amputation?"

"Yes, are you ready?"

"Who are they?"

"Yankees. What the hell they're doing here is beyond me, but here they are."

"Well, I'm ready."

"Let's get this over with, then." They returned to the room and found two burly soldiers waiting along with the Captain. "This is Mary, my assistant.

While we are in this room performing this operation, you and your men will do what she says when she says it. No more, no less. Has he had whiskey?"

"A cupful."

"Good. Let's begin. Mary."

With that, Mary motioned a soldier to either side of the table, laid out the necessary implements from the amputation bag and spread a cloth on the floor to receive the limb. She then caused the young soldier to lie back, placed a wooden block under his head, soaked some gauze in what little chloroform remained, and held it over the soldier's mouth and nose. "Breathe deep now, child, breathe deep. Won't hurt none at all."

Rush spoke to those gathered around the table. "Time is crucial. This man's chances of survival are directly related to how long the surgery takes. With that in mind, I cannot have him thrashing about. I do not know how long the anesthesia will last. Hold him and hold him tight." The two soldiers nodded and laid hold of their comrade.

Lifting the leg a few inches off the table and flexing it at the knee as best he could, Rush made ready to cut. Clutching the knife fully in his hand as opposed to holding it like a pencil, he expertly drew it through the muscles atop the leg. Then, reversing the blade end up, he repeated the procedure underneath, drawing the bloody instrument towards him, making use of all available leverage to cut deep. The soldier opposite him fell to the floor in a heap as an artery began spurting blood.

"Captain, quick, move that man aside and take his place—hurry!" Captain Anderson had just assumed his new station when the patient began to scream and convulse with pain. "Hold him, hold him!" Rush grabbed his saw and began grinding the teeth against the pristine bone. A mere two minutes later he was through and the fetid leg fell to the floor. Working with renewed determination, he tied off the bleeding and sewed up the skin flaps. Sinking into a chair, the exhausted doctor, who had already put in an eighteen-hour day, asked for whiskey himself. Mary brought him a glass half full. "Now we wait," he said to no one in particular. "Now we wait and pray and see. Captain, he is to rest here tonight, keep a man with him. I suggest that one on the floor."

"I agree." The Captain then kicked the prostrate private, reviving him. Gathering his sword and hat, the young officer turned to Rush. "Thank you, Doctor, thank you."

Leaning on Mary for support, Rush made his way out. Before exiting, he glanced back at the bloody table, the one-legged man, and the severed appendage lying still and white on the floor. "We shall see, Captain, we shall see. Perhaps we were in time."

Chapter 27

Colonel McElroy swung back the flap on Leander's tent, nodded to Othello, and called Captain Liner to the evening's onerous duty. A Lieutenant Spivey of the 22nd North Carolina has been tried by court-martial and convicted of cowardice at the Battle of Gaines Mill. The entire brigade had been brought out for evening parade and formed up in the shape of a hollow square. Lieutenant Spivey was escorted to the center of this enclosure. A sentence of dismissal in disgrace from the army was then read. The adjutant general then took the offending officer's sword from him and broke it over his head. His pistol was broken and the pieces scattered. The buttons and shoulder straps were cut off and discarded. Details of his disgrace were ordered published in all the newspapers where his regiment was raised. A placard marked "coward" was hung around his neck, and guards, two preceding him with muskets at reverse arms and two following, holding fixed bayonets to his back, marched him off. The lieutenant was to serve out his enlistment at hard labor, forfeiting any pay or allowances.

In this manner then, the men were admonished as to the rewards awaiting those who shirked their duty.

Captain Liner reclined on the remnants of an old horse blanket, close by a small fire Othello had built next to their tent. At long last the rains had stopped, and they had managed to swap a cigar for a brace of squirrel, which constituted supper that night. Othello was reading to Leander from their favorite play, *Hamlet*. They passed a small demijohn of brandy between them.

"You know, Othello, I just can't understand how people make Polonius out to be such a fool. Perhaps he had outlived his usefulness in the political realm, but his admonitions to Laertes alone rank with the great insights. How say you?"

"You mean 'these few precepts'—there?"

"Yes, turn to those."

Othello found the passage straight away in his practiced manner. He read from the worn and soiled yet cherished volume. "And these few precepts in thy memory, look thou character, give thy thoughts no tongue, nor any unproportioned thought his act. Be thou familiar, but by no means vulgar. Those friends thou hast and their adoption tried...."

"There—that alone—'those friends thou hast *and their adoption tried,*' 'if they have been through the fire with you,' 'grapple them to thy soul with hoops of steel.'" The two looked at each other as men are wont to do, deep in their belief of what had been read, and equally glad another, more eloquently spoken man had said it.

"Please, go on."

"'But do not dull thy palm with entertainment of each new-hatch'd, unfledged courage. Beware of entrance to a quarrel; but, being in, bear't that th' opposed may beware of thee. Give every man thy ear, but few thy voice; take each man's censure, but reserve thy judgement.'" Here Othello skipped the lines pertaining to clothes—he was intent on more important matters. "'Neither a borrower nor a lender be; for loan often loses both itself and friend, and borrowing dulls the edge of husbandry. This above all—to thine own self be true, and it must follow, as the night the day, thou canst not then be false to any man.'"

A silence came over them. Leander then said, "Well read, Moor, well read. I am somehow reminded of this; also from *Hamlet*—'a man may fish with the worm that hath eat of a king.'"

Nodding, Othello concluded the line, "'Why not imagination trace the dust of Alexander till a find it stopping a bung hole.'" They both managed a weak laugh as Leander looked into the fire and sifted some dirt through his fingers. "What is that—a 'bung' hole?"

Othello searched his memory.

"I think it was the opening in a cask." Leander stopped, realizing he had been rhythmically and methodically removing and replacing the cork in his flask. He turned the plug over slowly, examining the indentations and markings at length for any hint of its ancestry. He carefully replaced it, exchanging a glance with Othello, who was also privy to the symmetry of the moment. "Indeed, indeed," Leander uttered as he laid the flask down with a reverence that belied the dented and dingy tin container.

Chapter 28

Leander was immersed in the mind numbing administrative details that accompanied his role as company commander. He had welcomed the arrival of Captain Stowe, relieving him of his Battalion position. Stowe was a combat veteran, a Tar Heel, and a graduate of the Citadel. While he had enjoyed and learned from his brief tenure as second-in-command, Leander was the first to recognize and admit that he was not yet ready for the responsibility associated with leading several hundred men versus a Company. He would be, but not now. So intent was he on the minutia at hand that he remained unaware of the knocking on his tent post until it became both louder and more persistent.

"Yes, what is it?"

"Captain, a man here to see you."

"Well, who the hell is it, Sergeant? I asked not to be disturbed!"

"I know, sir, but this guy won't take no for an answer."

"Well, by God, show him in, I'll give him a lesson in no."

"Yes, sir." Leander returned to his paperwork, hoping to calm himself before the insistent intruder made his entrance. He heard the flap open, someone enter, and from the sequence of subsequent sounds, instinctively knew his visitor had come to attention.

"Captain Liner?" the disembodied voice asked.

Refusing to acknowledge the inquiry by looking up, Leander summoned his best officer's voice. "Yes, what is it?"

"Private Thomas Liner reporting for duty, sir."

Leander looked up and after an incredulous moment of recognition, sprang to his feet, knocking the makeshift table, accumulated papers, log book, rosters, diary, pencils, pocketknife, and unlit lantern all over the tent as he embraced his brother.

"Thomas! How… where… what… what in the world are you doing here?"

"Joined up, brother. Tried to make a go of it with the 62nd in Tennessee, but them boys fold too easy, so me and Traylor come up here for some real fightin'."

"Traylor?"

"You've heard of him. Traylor Crockett."

"Yes, yes, I have, but when, how did you come to… do Mom and Dad know? We have so much to discuss! Do they even know where you are?"

"I'll explain all that later. Where's Othello?"

"Out gathering wood. He'll be so happy to see you."

"And I him! Now I'd like you to meet Traylor and Sycamore."

"Who's that?"

"You'll see."

"Well, bring 'um in."

"That requires more discussion. Actually, I don't think they'll fit."

"Nonsense. Bring them in or I can come out."

"Maybe we'd better do that."

"OK. Let's go." The pair stepped outside into a bizarre gathering centered on two towering giants surrounded by curious gawking troops. Leander was also dumbfounded. "Good Lord, who made these two?" Sycamore saw this as his cue to enlighten the assembled masses.

"One God, Gentlemen, two colors. Sycamore Pin Oak, at your service. This little fella next to me is the famous Traylor Crockett. You got any problem with Sycamore, take it up with him. We come to whup a mess of Yankees, if that's all right with you, Boss. Any of 'um left worth shootin'?"

Leander stepped back, marveling at the sight evolving before him. Here were some fifty Deep South white men, who, if not actively dismissive of all Negroes, were certainly inclined through life, custom, culture, and habit to treat them as nonentities. Yet here were those same rough combat veterans standing in rapt attention, listening to a black hulk, nodding their heads in agreement, moving closer in, assuring their interrogator that yes, pickings were good when it came to shootin' Yankees. They even went so far as to reassure Sycamore that things being the way they were, usually one Southerner had his choice of two or three Federals to kill. They forgot, if only for the moment, that the dark embodiment of the deadly contest they were engaged in stood before them, and to actually enroll a Negro in the business of fighting Yankees was unheard of.

"All right men, assembly's over, return to your duties," Leander ordered. They turned, muttering, and left. These days, the men followed Leander's orders without hesitation. They had found it increased their chances of survival—a good thing. Of those remaining, Leander, Thomas, and Traylor sat. Sycamore, cognizant of his precarious stature, if no one else was, volunteered to help with any chores that needed doing. Leander was about to send him off to help Othello when he saw his "orderly" returning with an armload of locust, an axe hung through his belt.

Thomas, who had initially entertained thoughts of hiding and surprising Othello, could not, upon actually seeing his old friend, contain himself. He hurriedly rose and ran towards the at first startled, then puzzled, then overjoyed black man. Dropping his load, he and Thomas embraced, held each other by the shoulders, looked each other up and down, pronounced each other fit, then retrieved the scattered wood and rejoined the others who had been watching the reunion. Sycamore felt it incumbent upon himself to remark, "Dat's what I'm talkin' 'bout."

Through supper, cigars, and some brandy Leander had been hoarding, the five men talked until early morning, acquainting themselves with each other and the reasons they had all come together in this place at this time.

Chapter 29

Leander was successful in getting Thomas assigned to his company, and Traylor's reputation, which actually accompanied him to even these remote environs, assured him a posting as scout along with Daniel Daylight. This addition gave the 16th North Carolina two formidable pairs of eyes, ears, knowledge, and acumen. It was agreed that Sycamore would assist Othello. Indeed, it did not take long for the abilities inherent in the little group to make themselves known at Division level. When combined with Leander's prior successful flank scouting mission, they were the logical choice for another clandestine mission. This effort was of such import that none other than the commanding general himself, A.P. Hill, could relay the instructions. Having been summoned, the original scouting party plus Thomas and Traylor made their way with some trepidation to headquarters. Leander, Daylight, and Crockett were shown into Hill's tent by his adjutant. They found the fiery General clad in his white calico shirt knitted for him by his wife reclining on a cot, looking somewhat ashen.

"Gentlemen, please find a seat. I apologize for my sorry state. An indiscreet alliance while a youth continues to haunt me. Be forewarned… well, to the substance of why I called you. I have in my possession both important intelligence in the form of a map and captured Federal orders as well as bank drafts that must, and I stress must, be delivered to General Jackson tonight. I wish you to carry them to him. They must be delivered—at all costs—through the Federal forces separating our two armies. Do you understand my meaning, Captain?"

"I do, sir."

"Excellent. My adjutant will give you the materials as well as our best conjecture as to General Jackson's whereabouts. It is imperative you find him and place these in his hand only—by sunrise. Good luck and Godspeed."

Just prior to setting out, Othello and Leander exchanged glances as they were packing the saddlebags.

"Think we should tell him now?"

"Let's wait until we get back. I want him focused now."

"Understood."

However, as Thomas joined them and as an inducement to his brother, Leander said, "Thomas, when we get back from this little excursion, Othello has some news I think you'll favor."

Puzzled but intrigued, Thomas looked first at one, then the other. Discerning no clues from their close smiles, he relented. "OK, then. I look forward to this pronouncement."

"You will."

"You will," Leander echoed.

"I will," Thomas added as they all laughed easily.

With General Hill's authority behind him, Leander commandeered the best of everything he required. The band set out at dusk astride resplendent, trained cavalry horses armed with captured Spencer repeating rifles. As officer in charge, Leander made sure that every man understood that *not* being detected was of primary importance to the mission, and secondly, that everyone, including himself, was expendable in order to ensure success.

Three hours hard ride brought them up before the base of a range of mountains over which they had every right to believe Jackson was encamped. Equally certain was the knowledge that between them and "old Jack" were two full regiments of Federal cavalry. Sending Traylor and Daylight ahead, the rest of the party retired to the fringes of a bog that at the very least afforded them protection from incursions on three sides. There, silently, they waited.

A few minutes into this shared vigil, Thomas, as low man on this enlisted totem pole, went to fill their canteens in abeyance to the soldier's dictum that any water beats none and the new man goes to get it. As he knelt by the murky stream in the twilight, he noticed a small grotto hidden by ferns, from which clear water debouched into the other, brown runoff. Overcome with delight to have found a clean drink for his comrades, he thrust, at arms length, the first canteen in to fill. In that transient moment of reflection afforded by the cascading water and its attendant liquid melody, Thomas pondered the enigmatic conversation he had had with Leander and Othello. "Now, what 'news' has he got to tell me?" In the terror that followed, the youngest Liner wasn't sure if the knowledge that he had violated one of his own dictums preceded the smell registering through his nostrils—he had always maintained he could smell snakes—or if the sense of movement he detected from the periphery of his vision came first. In any event, he knew a mistake had been made, a significant one. He had used up his chance. The first water moccasin actually struck him in the eye, sinking its fangs into the orb of soft white tissue surrounding his pupil and partially separating the eye from its socket as Thomas instinctively jerked his head back. This action also served to expose his neck, where the second snake struck, puncturing the jugular and depositing venom directly into the bloodstream. The third and fourth serpent bit him on the arm and again in the face, but the damage had been done before their poisons began coursing through his body. After falling into the stream, he was barely able to stumble back into their makeshift camp. In hushed tones he told his brother what had happened. X's were immediately cut through those fang marks that lent themselves to this exercise and three men made to suck the venom out before applying tourniquets. It was in this state of affairs that Traylor and Daylight found them as they thundered back to camp.

"Captain, two Federal cavalry patrols right behind us, coming fast, one on the left, another on our right!"

"Muzzle the horses and let's get to the middle of this bog! Keep quiet! Our lives depend on it!"

They made their way through the muck and mire into the center of the swampy ground, forced the horses to lie down in an equine perimeter, and set up inside it as best they could for whatever eventuality came to pass.

The massive doses of poison in Thomas's veins coursed through him, reaching his brain and other vital organs in a matter of minutes. He began writhing, alternating between screaming and incoherent mumbling. The unmistakable sound of rapidly moving horses soon reached the enclave. Numerous attempts to quiet Thomas proved futile, even after binding him and stuffing a rag between his swollen lips. His strength and delirium overcame continued efforts to silence him. The sounds of advancing horsemen became more and more pronounced. Traylor and Daylight looked back at Leander in the partial moonlight, their eyes asking what their mouths could not frame. Leander understood their silent inquiry and answered by ordering "Eyes front," while the clambering cavalry still muffled his words to all but those immediate to their issuance.

The two Federal columns drew up on either side of the bog and dismounted. In the sudden and profound silence that now attended, Leander covered Thomas's face with his hand, smothering his brother.

This act transpired behind a concentric circle of twelve hardened men who peered out through the darkness into the miasma of war as rivulets of tears streamed down their encrusted faces.

Chapter 30

With the eventual passage of the Federal patrols, Leander's men secured Thomas's body across one of the horses and made for Jackson's headquarters. Although unspoken, the entire demeanor of the group had radically changed. They would no longer cower, nor hide, nor elude, nor avoid. The way now, the purpose was simple—point A to point B—and God help anyone or anything that lay in between. They were now possessed of, if not possessed by, a wrath born of sadness, futility, and rage. They carried their talisman across a saddle.

As they crested a gap atop the mountain, they met another Federal cavalry column. Leander raised his hand, stopping his party a mere ten yards from their adversaries, who had also halted, startled by the sudden encounter. Momentarily, only the pawing and snorting of horses, whose breath turned to white vapor in the rarefied air, broke the stillness. In this moment, it was as if the Confederate group manifested itself in a tangible, malevolent aura that surrounded them. Leander's counterpart looked across the ground, separating them into the eyes of the Rebel Captain and a chill ran through him not attributable to the temperature. As Leander's hand dropped, his men surged forward as one body, one scream. Minutes later, every Yankee soldier and horse lay dead.

The spectral, gray column continued down the trail. Their passage seemed preceded by an ominous foreboding, which parted their path like the bow of a ghost ship, sending every living thing scurrying from its wake. Those who take notice of such things would have seen the very flora drop their arms in obsequious reverence to the death dreadnaught making its way past.

They arrived at Jackson's camp without further incident. Their manner and countenance reflected the way they had come, for those who rose to meet them or greet them or challenge them melted away. The column drew up before Lieutenant General Thomas Jackson's tent. Without announcement or introduction, Stonewall came out, answering the silent invocation. It was possible Leander had brought his message and brother to the only man who understood his odyssey intuitively. Without a word, Jackson walked to

Thomas's body, lifted his head in both hands, and gazed at him. In spite of the swollen and distended face, he sensed the kinship. He turned to Leander.

"You were one?"

"Yes, sir."

"You will be again."

Leander dismounted, gave Jackson the bundled documents he had been entrusted with, turned, and began to walk away, his body racked with sobs.

Jackson addressed his adjutant. "Colonel, see to those men's needs and offer *Major* Liner a place at my table tonight."

Leander slipped into the dining tent as unobtrusively as possible and took the first seat available near the entrance. His arrival did not go unnoticed, however, and Jackson, at the head of the table, waved Leander to the place of honor on his right.

"General, I wish to thank you for my brevet promotion."

"You did your duty, however difficult. It was deserved."

"Perhaps. I'm unsure."

"Of the act, or the duty? I am not."

"I can't bring myself to write our parents."

"Then I will."

"No, please, I didn't mean to imply that you...."

"I will and consider it an honor to do it."

"Thank you."

"Do not let this cause you to question your faith, son."

"May I speak freely, General?"

"Of course."

"It's too late for that."

"May *I* speak freely?"

"General, you don't need my permission to...."

"In this instance, I do."

"Then, of course."

"Is the matter of concern to you because it was your brother? What of the other brothers, sons, and fathers? I believe, as I think you do, in what we are trying to accomplish here. Duty, sir, prevails. What of the thousands who have and will die following my orders? We must simply obey and leave it to a merciful God to rectify. No other way will work. Else, we presume. You did what had to be done—the duty supplants all. We must proceed on that basis, or our cause is blemished and we falter. I do not expect these words to alleviate your grief or doubt, but it is crucial you hear them."

Leander nodded, mesmerized by the conviction and crystal clarity of Jackson's eyes. Eyes that translated belief into vision. Eyes that radiated in battle. Clear, intense, sure, knowing eyes that now embraced him, and he felt the bonds that constricted his heart loosen.

Chapter 31

Sycamore found Othello storing some canned goods in a trunk around back of Leander's tent. He lowered his considerable frame to the ground, cut off a plug of tobacco, and offered some to Othello.

"Obliged."

"Is you a free nigger?"

"I am."

Sycamore considered this, eyed Othello, shifted his bulk, and asked, "You chooses to come here?"

"I did."

"Dat, like you say dat Shakespeare fella say, is passin' strange."

"I suppose. Yet it also shows how wrong it can be to lump everyone of a kind, color, into one idea of how they should be."

"Say what?"

"White men, most white men, look at coloreds one way. They see a slave, or at the very least, an inferior being, a lesser person. Conversely, the thought of a colored man being here because he wants to be don't fit the way we ought to think. No man should own another. No man owns me. Many other men own many more of my brothers. That is wrong. I suspect when this is over, it will no longer be, regardless of who wins. At the very least, it will no longer be official—the policy will change. The thing itself will go on in another guise. Someday, that too will change. Some other day, that change will itself change. Right now, my friend is here, and I want to be with him and he with me."

"Dat's what I am talkin' bout," Sycamore exclaimed.

"Say what?"

"Sycamore always said change come from in a man, not off a piece of paper. Not dat da paper ain't important, but da real change come inside. Ain't right for no man to own another but seem to Sycamore nuff blame to go round for dat one. I hear Uncle Abraham gonna give us the paper. Maybe dat will start da change, but Lord, it's gonna get worse fore it gets better."

"Thomas told me you were whipped."

"In front of my chillren."

"Now, see—there's one white man that needs killing. But you can't kill 'um all. That's as bad as saying all coloreds are dumb."

"I hated leaving more dan anything, but da shame on my baby's face was more dan I could stand."

"That I understand."

"One way or another, I'm gonna buy 'um out. Price done set, just gotta find da monies."

"If you do, we know some folks who'll serve as intermediaries." Sensing Sycamore's confusion, Othello went on to explain. "Helpers, people who will help you."

"Good, good! Dat helps Sycamore's heart! But—man, what done come over you? Da look on your face like you seed a ghost!"

Othello had risen, dropping the cans he held as he gazed southward at the approaching horsemen. Leander led the group, followed by Traylor, whose Percheron carried both him and a body, wrapped in canvas, across its flanks. Othello knew without looking whose body it was. Leander drew up in front of his tent. Othello looked first at him, then at the shroud, his imploring gaze going back and forth between the two. Leander merely nodded in answer to the mute question. "Get the Chaplin and give Private Liner a proper military burial." Several members of the party rode off in search of the Chaplin.

"Othello, if you would, if you can, I would appreciate your bathing Thomas and putting some fresh clothes on him. I need to report to General Hill."

Othello moved to help Traylor untie the body. As they were doing so, Sycamore walked over, took the lifeless form in his corded arms and carried it, ever so gently, to Leander's tent.

After being debriefed by General Hill, Leander returned to his campsite to find everything in readiness for the funeral. He addressed those who had gathered.

"When my brother died..." He paused to let his breath catch up with his words. "When my brother died, the way he died, a line found its voice in my head: 'As flies to wanton boys, so are we to the gods, they kill us for sport.' Well, Thomas Liner was more than that. He was more than an accidental cosmic utterance, a moment's note snuffed out by fate. He was my brother, my friend, a soldier, a son, a man. May God keep, love and honor him as we do. Amen."

A chorus of 'amen' echoed around the grave site, which had been chosen on a slight rise behind the encampment. It faced south. Then, a singular 'amen' sounded from behind the group. Turning they saw General Hill astride his horse replace his hat and ride off.

Back in his tent, Leander asked Othello to secure him a couple hours sleep and then summon Sycamore. The newly promoted major woke from a fitful sleep punctuated by dreams of his mother undergoing agonizing labor pains only to bring forth a writhing mass of snakes in a pool of blood. He welcomed Othello's call to rise. After washing off in a basin, he called for both Othello and Sycamore to come in. Sycamore stood, hunched over, hat in hand.

"Major, please accepts my sincere sorrys on da death of your brother. I knows he was more dan kin to you."

Leander's countenance expressed surprise at this utterance, or at least its form.

"I never cease to be amazed, despite my resolve not to. Sycamore, how much do you think it will take to buy your family out?"

"Don't think—know. Seven-hundred fifty U.S. dollars."

"Here's eight in greenbacks, use and guard it well."

"God Almighty, Boss, where dis come from?"

"From the monies we took to General Jackson—and don't you two start—this was done with his knowledge. I told him I had good use for eight hundred of what we brought him. 'An unusual request from an unusual soldier,' he says. 'Is it for pecuniary gain?' he says. 'No,' I say. And then raising his arm up over his head like he was giving absolution or asking a blessing, he closes his eyes and asks, 'Will it be employed in a manner so as to further the Lord's work?' 'Yes,' I answer. 'Take it,' he says."

"Oh, God, what a blessing, I say! Merciful Lord, an answer to my prayers!"

"Othello can give you a letter to friends who will help? I wish you and your family the best, Sycamore. Take care."

"Never in my life, Boss, have words failed Sycamore Pin Oak. But all I can say is thank you, thank you."

They shook hands as Othello and Sycamore made to sit down and compose the letter.

Chapter 32

Leander took up his long gun, mounted Horse, and trailing a pack mule, went hunting. This, a conscious effort to inject some normalcy into the chaos of his recent life.

He rode high into the ageless mountains following barely visible game runs until the sound, sight, and smell of the army were far behind and below him. He came out of a grove of hemlocks onto a heath bald about two acres in size. The grass lay like an emerald rug across the undulations of the ancient ground beneath.

He unsaddled his mount and hobbled the mule in reach of a spring that emerged beneath a lichen-covered boulder. Man and beasts drank long and deep of the clear, bracing water. Leander laid the saddle down on a small mound, threw his blanket over it, rested his head in the seat, and looked out over green and blue hills running to the sky. The sun dove in and out of a mute armada of pure white clouds as big as the mountains they drifted over. Gradually, the sun's rays permeated to his very core, warming and healing. The melodic interplay of wind, trees, and birds induced a complete, utter, deep, undisturbed slumber.

He awoke, hours later, a different man than the one who had fallen asleep. He sensed, without looking, that he was no longer alone. Maybe it was the barely perceptible sound, a soft munching like grass being pulled and nibbled. Slowly turning his head, he saw no less than twenty deer grazing across the clearing. He sat up, and their only reaction was to raise their heads and watch him. One old buck hobbled on three good legs, and Leander knew that was the one he would cull. Amazingly, as he raised his gun to fire, the herd turned to look at the elder statesman as if they too knew he was the rightful object of the hunt. One shot, the rest ran and the old monarch fell, dead.

An hour later, Leander had him field dressed and slung across the mule. He slowly made his way back down from his high sanctuary, promising himself to return if possible. As he negotiated a particularly steep and sharp portion of the trail, his horse coughed, reared its head, and stopped. Looking to his right in response to a muffled snorting sound, Leander stared into the grizzled face of a boar hog that had been rooting in the bank not an arm's length away. The dirt and debris turned up by its excavation mingled with an abundance of saliva and dripped round the enormous tusks onto the upturned earth.

Momentarily startled, Leander was clueless as to his next move. Then, slowly, he removed his revolver from his belt, lifted it even with the beast's face and fired, point blank. A hellacious high-pitched scream followed, and the hundred pound hog rolled off onto the trail. A difficult field dressing followed on the narrow trail as Leander stopped several times to calm his skittish horse. Finally, he had the swine secured along with the deer across his mule. He washed the dried metallic blood off his hands and resumed his trek back to camp, sure in the knowledge of a grateful reception from men who had been subsisting on parched corn for over two weeks.

Chapter 33

As Traylor's massive frame strode back into their campsite, Leander noticed he was holding his stomach while tears streamed down his weathered face. What, he thought to himself, short of an entire Union Corps and a few denizens of Mt. Olympus could have wrought such havoc on Traylor Crockett? Then he saw his huge companion was near to convulsing with laughter.

"Traylor, what is it?"

Gathering himself, Traylor sat, or more accurately fell, to the ground like a giant redwood, took a long drink from his canteen and somewhat fitfully, began. "You know Bull Bateman?"

"Yes, I think so. Fella over in the 13th?"

"That's him. Well, Bull's a fine fella, ceptin' when he gets in his cups, and then...."

"Then he's got to show everybody his dick."

"Right!" Traylor began to convulse again. "Well, he'd had a few nips and wanted to bet anybody in this man's army a sack of coffee and two dollars his was the biggest around. Fellas started running back to their companies to grab up their studs and bring 'em back. Well, everybody gathered round and Bull whips his out. Now, don't get me wrong, Bull's well endowed and proud of it. 'Hold on!' this fella from the 22nd says. 'You might as well put that paltry thing up, son,' and out he pulls one half again as big. I mean to say 'cries of adulation,' as my daddy use to say, went around those gathered. This ol' boy starts to reach for the winnings when Monk Mann steps up. You know him?"

"No."

"Little fella over in the 38th. Maybe five feet and a hundred pounds, soaking wet. 'Here, boys,' he says, 'try this on for size.' Well, he hauls out a dick that would send Traveler back to the barn. I thought he would never finish pulling that thing out of his britches. God knows where he stores it, much less how he walks around. He lets folks amaze at that awhile, takes another five minutes putting it up, gets his coffee and money and walks off. Funniest thing I ever saw, that look on Bull's face."

"And this Monk such a little fella."

"Yea, Cuz, but he's all dick," snorted Traylor as both he and Leander rolled laughing on the ground.

Chapter 34

Like other women of her time and, in particular, of her place, Rebecca could not afford the luxury of indulging her anxiety or giving free rein to her worry. Survival, in a very real sense of the word, dictated her actions from sun up to dark, and often well into the night.

Levi had left before daylight the previous day to help a neighbor bring in his hogs that had been free-ranging. He did so because it was the right thing to do, and usually, in these circumstances, a ham was offered in gratitude.

A destitute, sickly soldier on healing-leave returning home to Tallulah Falls, Georgia, stopped by the Liner house to deliver a letter and beg a drink of water.

"This the Liner place?"

"Yes, it is."

The gaunt soldier lifted his worn hat and looking at the ground beneath Rebecca's feet said, "Jacob Priest, Ma'am, from Georgia. I'm on my way home for a spell and was asked to deliver this letter." He pulled a tattered envelope from his shirt and offered it to Rebecca. Her initial elation and gathering smile fell when she did not recognize the handwriting.

"Do you know what this is?"

"No, Ma'am, but I've carried two others and none was good. Sorry."

Rebecca's insides seized up, wondering which one it was, or, oh God, was it both.

"For what it's worth, Ma'am, that one was written by old Jack himself."

"Who—Old Jack?"

"Stonewall, Ma'am. Stonewall Jackson."

Rebecca found herself considering whether notoriety or rank made death any more palatable and then hated herself for doing so. "Well, thank you, Mr. Priest. Can I offer you anything?"

"Couple of apples would sure help, Ma'am. Can't keep much else down. And a little water."

"Certainly. Help yourself. That Horse Nose tree there has plenty left. Get all you want. The spring runs under the road. You'll see the gourd."

"Much obliged, Ma'am. Better git on now."

"Thank you again." She took the letter and sat in a rocker on the porch. After a deep breath, she opened it.

April 5, 1863

Dear Mr. And Mrs. Liner,
It is with the utmost sorrow that I write to inform you of the untimely death of your son, Thomas. Of all the responsibilities that befall me, this is the most difficult. The loss of a loved one, especially one so young, is a grievous burden. Having lost a son myself, I know that words cannot heal the pain of such a tragic event.
Your son died in the performance of his duties, an honorable and fitting end for any soldier. Leander, for whom I have the greatest admiration and affection, was with Thomas when he passed. I know this was a comfort for your son, as it must be for you.
Take strength from our Lord, whose love passeth all understanding.
I remain,
Your obedient servant,
Thomas L. Jackson
Lieutenant General, Commander 2nd Corps
Army of Northern Virginia, CSA

She was surprised at her own reaction, or more accurately, lack of one. Shock, yes, but not so profound as to deny reality. Thomas was dead—her son was gone. She would grieve with Levi, but also knew he would need her in order to make it himself. In the quiet, perhaps in the dark, certainly when alone, she would grieve as only a mother can for a child.

Levi returned whistling and carrying two sacks over his shoulders. They had found more hogs than expected, and each ham had already been salted and placed in burlap, ready to hang in the cave. He saw the letter lying on the kitchen table as he deposited the hams there. He glanced at Rebecca for understanding and saw in her face the loss.

"Thomas, Levi, it's Thomas."

He slumped in a chair, fingering the envelope as if not reading the contents would change them. Finally, he removed the single piece of paper and read.

When he had finished, he folded the paper, returned it to the envelope, stood and retrieved the family Bible. He recorded Thomas's death, placed the envelope within its thin worn pages, and returned it to the shelf. He held his arms at his sides and looked at Rebecca.

"What do we do?"

She crossed the room, took him in her arms and they cried—for Thomas, for themselves, and for each other. It took a while.

Chapter 35

An undercurrent of anticipation and excitement ran through the army unlike any Leander had seen before. They were going to cross the Potomac and march into Maryland.

"'Bout damn time," seemed to be the prevailing sentiment. "Let 'um see what it's like to war on their front porch." "Plenty of grain and food over thar."

Lee was understandably concerned with the Federal garrison at Harpers Ferry, which would be in his rear and along his line of communication once in Maryland. He therefore ordered General Jackson to take his troops and invest the strategic town. Once done, he was to rejoin Lee as soon as possible. Early on September 15th, Jackson had the place surrounded and began an artillery bombardment. Around nine that morning, the Federal commander, Colonel Miles, surrendered. Leander was ecstatic, casualties were minimal, and the prisoners would total over twelve thousand. As he rode along and behind Jackson when he entered the garrison, he overheard some of the Yankee soldiers who had lined the road to catch a glimpse of Stonewall. "Well, boys, he ain't much to look at, but if we had him, we wouldn't be in this fix."

"Where is he? Where is he? *That?* That's Stonewall Jackson? God, he looks like a derelict on a nag."

After accepting the surrender, Jackson quickly gathered his troops—excepting A.P. Hills—and made for Sharpsburg. Neither Hill nor Leander thought much of paroling all these prisoners, but it had to be done, and they were ordered to do it. On the 17th, they made ready to leave when a courier came from Lee on a horse so lathered none who looked on the poor beast could fail to sense the urgency of its mission. Hill put his men into a forced march that rivaled anything Leander had experienced. Heretofore, men laughed at being dubbed Hill's "Light Division" by saying, "Yea, light—cause he don't allow us to carry nothin' but a gun and rations." But this, this put to shame anything they had been through. And yet, it was that very sense of urgency that made them understand how important it was. The 16th, along with the rest of Hill's division, arrived at Antietam around 4:30 that afternoon and attacked Burnside's left flank. They would save Lee's army.

Three days later, Hill addressed his men in words that Leander would remember, verbatim, the rest of his life.

"Soldiers of the Light Division, you have done well and I am proud of you. You have fought in every battle from Mechanicsville to Shepherdstown, and no one can yet say that the Light Division was ever broken. You held the left at Manassas against overwhelming numbers and saved the army. You saved the day at Sharpsburg and at Shepherdstown you were elected to face a storm of round shot, grape and shell such as I have never before witnessed. Your services are appreciated by your commanding officer." So simple, so brief, and Leander was so proud.

Letters Home

September 20, 1862

dear maw,
we have been in a terribul battle here. we fit manful but truth to tell hit was most a draw. more an half our cannon shot is duds and these here ol muskets aint much account less you whop someone up side the head and i done that two. this place we call sharpsburg and they say it is antitum. oh ma the death and dying and hurtin and injuree is awful and i am sad to say we get use to it and do not pay it no mind but pile up boys that was your friends and shoot from behind um. this war is a thing no one knowed it would be. i am grazed some but hunger and wore out feet is worse. have you heered from Jonah. i got gun butted in the head and don't think rite like i use to. i no this is a worry to you but also you had druther no this than nothing. we got us a yank who give up. he asks me where i hail from. North Carolina i say. i no that he says pointin at our flags. whur he says. high lonesome i tells him and a lump comes to my throat. strange name he says. well fella i says where you come from. lick skillet ohio he says and puffs up. now maw, there fellas aint got no manners even when caught and where does a fella from lick skillet get off makin light of high lonesome. anyway we are all in good spirits considerin and the 16th is a good bunch. tell everbody I am fine and please send me a tung of leather for shoes and some coffee if u can.
  your loving son,
  Siler

Chapter 36

A physically exhausted and emotionally drained Leander Liner fell to his blanket beside Othello.

"What is today?"

"September—ahhh—19th, I think."

"Have you heard of the fighting at the Mule Shoe, the Bloody Angle?"

"They say it was the worst of the war."

"It may well have been. A dubious honor, but it may have been. I thank God all we had to contend with was Burnside on the eastern salient. I have spoken to some who were there. They still have that distant stare about them. Men became animals, something altogether foreign to even a soldier's nature. They grappled with each other by hand, with clubs, stomping their own dead and dying underfoot in the mud and blood and no one would relent. Ten thousand casualties on each side. Dear God, what have we become?"

Othello recalled a line Rebecca had read them from Shakespeare's *Caesar*. "'Cry havoc and let slip the dogs of war.'"

Leander nodded, also remembering. "They are loose, Othello, they are loose upon this earth."

Chapter 37

The 16th next marched to Bunker Hill and remained in camp there until October. The respite was welcomed by all but was not to last long because the Federal forces crossed the Potomac and advanced to Warrenton. Longstreet confronted them near Culpepper Courthouse, and on the 20th, Jackson abandoned the valley above Winchester and moved to New Market, thence to Guinea Station. Leander surmised that Fredericksburg would witness the next major clash, and so it proved to be, when on the 12th, Burnside began crossing the Rappahannock. The battle was joined on the next day and found, inexplicably to Leander, the 16th assigned to the edge of a gap in the Confederate lines some 200 yards wide. The Yankees were not fools and sought on several occasions to avail themselves of this fault. Leander and the rest of the 16th repulsed several assaults until reserves were brought up to plug the gap. And then, just as Leander was privately admiring their tactics, the Federal forces made assault after piecemeal assault on the Confederate lines, losing themselves in the effort. It was a damming, deadly example of poor generalship and would result, the Rebels would learn later, in the replacement of General Burnside by Hooker.

Like weary yet game and proud pugilists, the two armies separated to rest and replenish. As had been the case many times heretofore, the most the Army of Northern Virginia could squeeze out of the situation was rest. There was not a lot of replenishment to be had for Lee's warriors. "It's like the mythical Hydra, Othello—we cut off its head and it just grows more. Our men and animals are frequently famished, and then I read this in a northern paper."

"What?"

"An innocuous article detailing the fact that the rowing team at Yale has not missed a practice or competition since this war began. Good God, Othello, we give our last drop, and they row. How do you defeat a host like that? How?"

"I heard someone asked General Jackson much the same thing at Fredericksburg."

"What did he say?"

"Kill them, kill them all."

Silence fell between them.

"We will have to, we will. If they will not let us be, we will have to cut out their hearts as they pull and chant." Both men grew quiet, and then by mutual, unspoken agreement, fell to their blankets and sleep.

Letters Home

December 15, 1862

Dear James,
I want to tell you what goes on here in hopes you will give up any thought 'bout joining. I don't know nuthin bout heroes and glory but I do have a feel for combat or 'seeing the elephant' as soldiers say. Mostly you're scared to death. Getting to the fight you see way off the smoke from all its cannon. Then you hear the loud boom of the cannon and thousands of reports from muskets. If it's been goin' on a while you pass through the field hospitals, this is the wurst of all. Row after row of dead are on all sides. Arms and legs without bodies are everywhere. Men screaming and crying, many mangled so bad they don't look like men no more and mules and horses writhin' on the ground. Fellers do different sorts of things, some get real quiet, others joke loud. Many throw down cards and dice and naked woman pictures so's they won't wind up being sent home if you die. Some who ain't been through this before run and hide, some get sick. Some of those who have done it before pray and look within themselves. Now we form up, the drums beat and the flags are unfurled and we advance. It never seems to be fair weather for dying, it's always hotter than blazes or colder than a well digger's ass. You can't hardly breathe for the smoke or see. Faces get black with grime as you bite off cartridge after cartridge. Many a time I've shot so much my barrel is too hot to touch. Everywhere is noise and death. Before long water runs out and a thirst settles on you like none you've ever

known. If you make it through this part you've done up fer, can't hear and many fall asleep where they are. Others go looking for friends and comrades. This is it, Jim, don't do it. Stay home and help Ma and Pa and take care of sister, they need you, we don't. One dying is enough.

Your Loving Brother,
Lawrence

Chapter 38

A solitary violin drew out a mournful, evocative tune that drifted like wood smoke over the Confederate encampment, affecting men in as many different ways as there were those who heard it. Perhaps it was the unnatural stillness of the night, perhaps it was the bitter cold that permeated it, perhaps the simple fact that it was Christmas Eve served to make each note all the more poignant as men looked within themselves and remembered times not defined by fighting and death and the rigors and hardship of war.

Slowly, there arose, from the Federal forces in winter quarters across the river, strains of "The Bonnie Blue Flag." In response to this unexpected serenade by the enemy, the Rebel musicians gathered and played "Just Before the Battle Mother" for their foes. This exchange lasted through three more songs. As it ended, and, as if they were responding to the same baton, both sides took up the playing of "Silent Night."

As the last mutual note spent itself in the cold quiet air, men who had, and would again, kill those opposite, sobbed at the utter inherent cruelty of their undertaking, contrasted it with the feelings evoked by the song, and were grateful for the darkness that enveloped them.

Chapter 39

Almost three full months later, the army began movement towards Chancellorsville. Hooker had stolen a march on Lee and flanked him. Leaving 10,000 troops at Fredericksburg, Lee took 50,000 to contend with Hooker's 73,000. Fighting on the 1st of May was inconclusive. At supper that night, Leander noticed Othello was somewhat sullen and withdrawn. "What ails you, Dark Moor?" This inquiry brought a brief smile to his friend's face, but he soon fell to reflection again. "Othello, what is it?"

"Nothing, just silly superstition."

"Tell me, tell me."

"Old Negro man over in the 18th, their cook, threw bones last night."

"Ah. What did they say?"

"Something great and something bad, very bad, will come of this battle."

"And you believe him?"

"What was it Hamlet told Horatio?"

"'There are more things in Heaven and Earth than are dreamt of in your philosophy.'"

"Yes, I believe that."

"Me, too. But we shall just have to do our duty and let the bones fall where they may."

"Yes," Othello said, laughing in spite of himself. "Yes, we will."

May 2nd saw the definition of audacity redefined yet again as Lee sent Jackson and some 26,000 men round the right flank of the Union army while he remained to confront the original 73,000 with only 20,000 of his own. Leander sensed the momentous daring of the move as the 16th joined the rest of the 2nd Corp in the fourteen mile march. It was an utter rout as Howard's troops fell back some two miles before darkness stopped the Confederate pursuit. The great part, which had been foretold, had come about. Leander was reorganizing his men when a courier came with a message for J.E.B. Stuart, who was nearby. Stuart ordered the 16th to accompany him as he mounted and rode off in the direction the courier had come. All three of the 16th's top officers, McElroy, Stowe, and Lee, had been wounded, so Leander and

Captain Cloud assumed command. His own comrades, men of the 18th North Carolina, had wounded Jackson. The bad had come to pass also. Stuart took command and fought well. On the 3rd, both Confederate wings massed their artillery at a place called Hazel Grove and broke the Federal line, but the bad prognosticated by the tumbling bones was not over. A.P. Hill was also wounded and when, on the 10th, Leander learned of the passing of Jackson, he and many others wept openly and unashamedly.

"Othello, we have lost something in this army that I do not believe can be replaced. We will fight, and we will fight well, but I fear a part of our very soul died with that man."

Letters Home

My Dearest Alice,
I take pen in hand to let you know I am good. I mean I ain't been shot yet or anything but oh Alice I am so tired. I am tired of being tired. I am tired of being cold and hungry and wet. I wonder anymore what has become of me that I can nap before a battle, choose a man from among others and kill him and choose another. I am weary of being hot and thirsty, so much so that everything else don't count, even the want to live. I am tired of marching here and then back there. I grow tired of loud and profane men who will not bathe but walk miles for a pint of bad whiskey. I wish to God he had never made flies. Oh, Alice, the filth, you cannot escape it. The men will not use the latrines but squat anywhere. The cooks slaughter animals and throw the offal down. Pigs and dogs and flies and maggots infest everything. We kill each other like wheat before the scythe and burn trains of supplies after we get our fill and yet more come. Where do all these men and supplies come from? I sometimes wonder if God is on our side. I often wonder if he cares. You member Uriah Birdsong from Graham County? He was shot last month at Chancellorsville, lasted a day after losing his leg and passed. So many die, so many are injured and we ain't got no more to take their place. The yanks they just grow more, it is a wonderment. I fear we will not prevail. What then? Oh, Alice, I long to be with you at home and yet we go on and I will to.
Your Loving Husband,
Charles

P.S. Please try to find some hard rock candy and send it to me. It slacks the thirst. Send it to the usual address but note we move toward Fairfield Pennsylvania, near Gettysburg.

Chapter 40

Around the middle of June, Lee again decided to take the war into the enemy's countryside. Food, politics, and generalship drove his decision. The 16th crossed the Potomac at Shepherdstown on the 25th. The Confederate army stretched some twenty miles on either side of the river as it made its laborious way into Maryland. Its reception by the residents was indifferent at best and often outright hostile. Those who expected storybook soldiers were sorely disappointed. The gaunt, shabby, smelly members of Robert E. Lee's army of Northern Virginia met few of the criteria associated with conventional warriors. Most were threadbare, many wore no shoes, and they all stank. Man after man, company after company, regiment after regiment picked, probed, and gouged, removing vermin from their persons. And yet, there was something about them—an esprit, an assurance, and air that belied equipment or hygiene. These were the veterans, the distillation of battle. Gone were the shirkers, the cowards, the malingerers, the sunshine patriots. These were hard men, wedded to Lee, accomplished soldiers who knew how to fight, how to kill. They knew, *knew*, they were better than those they fought, better in battle than "those people." Thus, while their reception was not what many had anticipated, it was just one more thing—one more thing to deal with, one more thing to overcome.

Leander's company was reflective of the army as a whole. While his strength was roughly half what they started with, those remaining were seasoned men who knew their jobs and performed well under pressure. In short, Major Liner was proud of his men and they of him. He had their trust and confidence, they his. To the uninitiated then, the rabble filing past did not appear especially menacing or dangerous, and the taunts and jeers hurled at them reflected this misconception.

"You boys better remember your way, cause you'll be going back soon."
"Johnny Reb, you sure are a poor lookin' lot."
"Where's the real army, boys?"
The men took it all good-naturedly, smiling and waving to the crowds.
An army on the move is an immense undertaking. Once through Maryland

and into Pennsylvania, the main body split into three, taking different paths to facilitate movement as well as the dispersal of a potential target, yet remaining close enough to coalesce should the need arise. Leander, too, after consulting with his regimental commander, led several companies on a still different route towards the night's bivouac in order to facilitate foraging. They camped near the small hamlet of Fagotville on the 27th. As the armies converged on Gettysburg, the 16th was in Scale's brigade, Pender's Division of A.P. Hill's 3rd Corp. Leander saw first action when his division reinforced Heth on the Union left. Together, the two divisions renewed an attacked begun earlier by Heth. At about the same time, Ewell's troops, coming south from Carlisle, joined with Rodes division and attacked the Union center. When Jubal Early arrived from York, he succeeded in outflanking the Union right, and the Federals withdrew in disorganized fashion, back through Gettysburg. Leander was given to understand that two additional Federal Corp under Sickles and Slocum had arrived, and the Union army dug in south of the town.

Chapter 41

Lee had issued specific and firm orders regarding pillaging and confiscation of property. It was deemed important not to further alienate the populace. His orders were to obtain provisions, if possible, adhering to standing orders by paying for it in Confederate script. With this in mind, Traylor had returned from a brief foray into the countryside to announce that a farmhouse, situated over a hill to the left of their march, was abundantly provided with grain, water, and animals. Leander then drew monies from the bursar, turned over command to his second, requisitioned a wagon and team, then struck out for the cornucopia Traylor had described. He declined on purpose an escort, maintaining his chances were better alone and unthreatening.

Topping the hill, he drew up in wonder at the sight before him. As one immersed in war, versed in death, and accustomed to land razed and denuded by fighting, the farm spread out below stood in such sharp contrast that it could have originated in a dream. The pastoral setting pulled at Leander, reminding him of home, not so much by its physical properties but by the sense of serenity pervading it. The fields, crops, and buildings could have been drawn by an old master, so perfect was their symmetry. As a farmer himself—God, it seemed like another time, another place—Leander marveled at the obvious care and thought that had gone into its planning, layout, and maintenance. He almost felt as if he would be violating some sanctity by pursuing his duty. Nevertheless, he roused himself, slapped the reins across the horse's backs, and proceeded down the road, across a rock bridge bearing the words *Bent Oak* at the ends of its arches and on through the Elysiuan fields to the farmhouse.

A long watering trough dominated the south end of a red, two-story dairy barn. It was ingeniously fed by two downspouts affixed to guttering running the length of the structure. Leander stopped the horses by the trough.

"Now, *that* makes sense," Leander said aloud.

"Yankee ingenuity," a voice sounded behind him.

Leander turned in the wagon seat, one hand holding the reins, the other, from habit, grasping the handle of his revolver. Had he needed to fire, he probably would have done so by aiming the reins, because now he lost all sense of the present as he looked at the most striking, statuesque, beautiful woman he had ever seen or imagined. The very air between them seemed charged as she held his gaze. Her resolute, unafraid resolve shown through brilliant steel gray eyes set atop pronounced cheekbones framed by luxuriant, long black hair. Her olive skin was tinged red by exposure to the sun. Her long proportioned fingers were dirty from real work. Indeed, her unusual attire of pants, boots and a long-sleeved, white collarless shirt rolled up past the elbows and unbuttoned at the throat, merely served to accentuate, by contrast, her classic beauty. The old, gaucho-like pants were cinched down to an impossibly small waist by a belt that's excess hung limply even after being passed through several extra loops.

Regaining some semblance of composure, Leander left the horses to drink and made to come down off the wagon, an endeavor simple enough in conception but difficult in execution when not properly attended to. Custom would dictate to look where he was going, but Leander could not take his eyes off the vision before him. As a direct result, he misplaced his foot on a spoke of the wagon and tumbled to the ground in a disheveled and embarrassed heap. Dust settled over him in a vain attempt to cover his comic transgression. He slapped his hat across his outstretched legs, adopted the petulant look of a recalcitrant child, and resigned himself to well-deserved ridicule. Instead, her laughter lifted his self-absorption and he joined with her in mutual appreciation of his faux pas.

"Well, Johnny Reb, if you're a true sample, this war is over."

Leander was somehow and suddenly possessed of boldness normally uncharacteristic of him. "I dare say, madam, that any man would fall down in your presence."

She eyed him, hands on those hips, trying to decipher this southern enigma.

"Well, be that as it may, what is it you require here?"

Leander stood, and with as much dignity as he could muster under the circumstances, addressed her inquiry, purposefully avoiding looking directly at her, lest he lose his way again. "Major Leander Liner at your service, Madam. I am authorized to procure provisions for our army."

"And how exactly does this 'procurement' work? Will you simply take what you want?"

"No, Ma'am, certainly not. We purchase it at fair market rates."

"With what, Confederate currency?"

"Why, yes, of course, of course."

"You might as well steal it—same thing."

"Madam, the Army of Northern Virginia in general, and myself in particular, does not steal nor make war on civilians. A practice, I might add, unlike that of the Federal forces."

"Well, Major, it seems obvious to even the casual observer that you intend to 'procure' from me. I cannot stop you, but know I would if I could. My father is an invalid and my uncle, who lives with us, is in the army—probably 'pillaging' as we speak."

Leander was taken aback and his voice showed it. "You... all this... you take care of all this?"

"Me and three 'free' blacks, Major. We do not enslave others."

Now Leander was riled, gender notwithstanding. "Nor do I, madam. May we discuss our requirements now and payments?"

"Yes, I suppose so. What choice is there? The porch would be more comfortable than standing here in the hot sun."

They moved towards the house and through a white picket fence surrounding it. As she opened the gate, Leander was again startled to find the yard surrounding the house to be grass instead of swept dirt. Neatly trimmed grass lined the stone walkway that led to the porch steps.

"I have never seen grass here, for this. It makes sense. More ingenuity, I assume."

She smiled despite herself, walked up on the porch and directed Leander to a large, comfortable rocking chair. "Sit here, and I will see to some tea."

"Thank you, that would be most welcome after my dust bath."

Again, she smiled, turned, opened the screen door, which provided access to the hallway, and called out, "Rose, bring us some tea on the porch please." From the recesses of the large house a voice responded, "Yes, Miss Summer. Be right out."

Leander rubbed the stubble on his chin, "Miss, huh? Well...." An eyebrow rose in acknowledgment. The vision-made-whole came back and sat down in another rocker next to Leander, who had risen as she did so.

"At least the war has not left you bereft of manners, Major."

"Manners, courtesy, a way of life—that is what some would say this war is about, Miss Summer...."

She seemed momentarily surprised that he knew her name, but quickly realized how he had come by it and the question inherent in his saying it. "I am Summer Will, Major, widowed two years, and that is nonsense. This war is about slavery, nothing else."

"You are partially right, madam. Yes, slavery, which I abhor, is a reason, but not the only one. To think so, pardon my bluntness, is simplistic, naïve, and does the South a great disservice."

"The South, sir, has done itself a great disservice by inaugurating and perpetuating such a vile institution."

"We did not inaugurate it, madam, but yes, we have done ourselves a great injustice by sustaining it."

Her eyes widened at this admission, and she studied, unashamedly, the face of the man who had said it. They gazed at each other across a distance of not more than two feet. Volumes passed between them, devoid of any words to carry it. The silence was broken by the screen door slamming closed as Rose, an enormous colored woman, brought out a service tray laden with tea. She placed it on a small table next to her mistress. Having done so, she gave Leander the once-over, shook her head, muttered, "Lawd, Lawd," and retreated to her lair deep in the bowels of the house.

"She likes you, Major, and I... I must admit, am intrigued myself."

Leander was not himself and did not care that he was not. Those who brush death and do not know their allotted hours discard formalities. "Madam, I am not only intrigued by you, but know—knew the moment I saw you—that I loved you. I am aware, painfully so, of how bizarre this must sound, but I do not have the luxury of protocol or etiquette. I will drink this, ask for your hand in marriage, and then go."

"Sir, you presume! How dare you! My hand in marriage! Indeed! Go you will!"

"I'll take that as a 'no.' Good day, madam."

Leander put his tea down, stood, placed his hat firmly on his head, wondered what in the hell had come over him, and walked down the steps to his wagon. He clambered up, seated himself, took the reins, and pulled the team round. His path took him past the porch where an agitated young Miss Will stood.

"Major, if you would be so good as to return tomorrow, we may conclude our business." She turned and went into the house.

Leander, having drawn the horses up, now queried them. "Well, what in the hell did that mean?"

As soon as the screen door closed, it opened again as Rose ambled out to fetch the tray. She stopped at the railing, looked Leander up and down again, shook her head again muttered, "Lawd, Lawd," again and went in.

Agreeing, Leander too muttered, "Lawd, Lawd," and drove off, intent on, if nothing else, returning.

Chapter 42

"Othello, ahhh... reckon you could boil the cooties out of this uniform?"

"I think so—the question is, why? They'll be back in a week."

"Well, just 'cause. I've got to go back tomorrow and get those provisions." They looked at each other through the still unanswered question hanging in the air between them. "And ahhh... maybe give me a haircut too, and a shave?" That answered it for Othello.

"Sure, Leander. What's her name?"

"Well *damn*. Summer Will. And Othello, I'm just lost."

"Sounds like you *found* something to me."

"Ha! Maybe so. It's all crazy, but what ain't these days?"

"Very little, but you know what they say, where there's a '*will*,' there's a way." They both dissolved into laughter, the rare kind afforded true friends.

Regaining his composure, Othello instructed his friend, "Now get those rags off and we'll try to make you presentable... Summer Will, huh?"

"I'm afraid Summer '*won't*.'"

"Well, '*will*' see."

That night and next morning, the company grapevine carried the news regarding their commander at an astonishing rate. Numerous unsolicited contributions from the men served to provide Leander with all the embellishments their impoverished state could manage. A mend here, some embroidery there, a cobbler contributes as does a former haberdasher, and soon Leander was resplendent, the end product rather imposing. Freshly groomed and refurbished, the mountain man cut quite a figure. Even Horse was given the once over when it was decided that Traylor would accompany him, driving the wagon. Thus Major Liner and Sergeant Crockett set off for the Will farm that afternoon.

Summer pushed the door to her father's room open with her hip as she balanced a tray in both hands.

"Dad, lunch."

John Henry Will looked over the top of his reading glasses and smiled as his daughter made her way to his wheelchair.

"Summer, you look quite fetching today."

"Why, thank you. It's just an old dress."

"You, my dear daughter, would look good in sack cloth and ashes."

"Oh, hush and eat. Rose has fixed your favorite."

"Prettier than a speckled pup under a red wagon."

"Hush now, I told you! Eat." As the senior Will began his meal, Summer sat down on the side of his bed, her hands folding and unfolding around one another.

"Dad, I need to discuss something with you."

"You mean that Confederate officer who came by yesterday seeking provisions?"

"Why yes, how did you know?"

"Rose told me of his visit."

"Oh, well then. What would you advise me to do?"

"About the provisions or the proposal?"

"Father! Did she tell you that, *too*?"

"No, merely raised the window so I could hear for myself."

"She *what*! You *heard*! The whole conversation?"

"All that mattered."

"Oh, Lord! I'm so embarrassed, and, Father, I'm so confused."

"Yes, it does seem to have had an effect on you."

"Yes, but I don't know what."

"We can figure that out later. What would you say to this young man if I wasn't here?"

"You taught me better than that. This is not a rhetorical exercise. You *are* here."

"True. Summer, you are my only child, my only... I was searching for a word, but that will do, 'my only.' Your happiness is all that matters to me. I think I know how you feel about this young man, but this is war, our country is at war with itself. It would be foolish to act as if that were not the awful reality. If you wish to join with this young man, I will not stop you, but I will ask that you do not do so until this business is finished. Will you indulge your father in this matter?"

"You are a wise and good man, and I love you. I will do it because you want it and because it makes sense for everyone involved. I want you to know that regardless of what I decide, no decision I contemplated entailed leaving you."

"I suspected as much."

"If... if yesterday was not an illusion, and he returns and if he still feels the same way, I'll inform him of the circumstances. If he accepts, then fine. If he does not, that too is fine."

"I think the answer to one of your musings is imminent, for if my remaining senses have not also abandoned me, I hear Rose's footsteps approaching in that rather unique manner of hers which indicate the urgent conveyance of vital information."

Indeed, Rose was hastening to Mr. Will's room, and as usual when she hastened anywhere, she outran one of her shoes and clip-clopped the rest of the way. "Miss Summer! Miss Summer! Here he come, here he come!"

"Thank you, Rose. Now please put on your other shoe, *close* this window, and bring some tea on the front porch." Chastised but unrepentant, Rose did as she was told, but not before exchanging winks with John Henry Will.

Leander drew up before the porch, dismounted and tied Horse to the hitching post. As he climbed the steps, Summer came out the door. When they looked at one another, the look was all, and all else dissolved. Movement stopped, as did their mutual breathing. She remained poised halfway out, holding the screen door. He stood still, one foot on the porch, one on a step. A moment passed by, a wealth of understanding passed between them. Then they breathed together, and made their still awkward way towards one another.

"Major Liner."

"Miss Will."

"I believe you require provisions."

"Sergeant Crockett has the list." Summer reluctantly swung her gaze in the direction Leander had mentioned, noticing Traylor for the first time. She sized up the man on the wagon, which took a while. Traylor nodded, smiled and removed his hat.

"Ma'am."

"Good Lord, if the rest are like him, Pennsylvania itself cannot provide."

"Don't fret, miss, I'm just a tad bigger than some and smaller than most."

"Heavens, you block out the sun! Give your list to Zeke there. He will assist you."

"Ma'am." Traylor called to the team, turning them, then moved off towards the barn and the waiting Zeke.

"Major, will you have some tea?"

"I am most grateful, Miss Will."

"For the provisions, or the tea?"

"Both, Ma'am, and the pleasure again of your company."

"I must say, Major, that you look very dapper today, but my company is a matter you will need to discuss with my father."

"An even greater pleasure, Ma'am."

"You haven't met my father, yet Major. I would reserve judgment until you do so."

"In this matter, I yield to your superior judgment."

"Oh, please, you haven't yielded to a woman your entire life."

"My dear *mother*, constantly. And besides, I haven't... I haven't in my entire life been in love, either."

"And you are now?"

"I am."

"With...?"

"You."

"Me?"

"You."

"Very well then... *Rose*! If I hear one more creak from that window I will thrash you personally!"

Leander thought he heard a distinctive clip-clop sound coming from inside the house. A partially subdued Rose brought out the tea service, placed it on a table between Leander and Summer, and made to go back in, but not before muttering a barely audible "Lawd, Lawd."

When they had finished their drinks, Summer asked if Leander was ready to meet her father.

"I am, but I readily confess, I do not feel this nervous even prior to battle."

"There I assume you *know* the enemy, Major."

"There I have no aspiration to *join* their side."

Summer escorted Leander into a large, well-furnished, first-floor corner room, which fronted the porch. Several windows admitted light from adjacent sides. A large four-poster bed had been placed against one wall. A distinguished middle-aged man devoid of facial hair occupied an ornate wooden wheelchair. A blanket draped across his lap fell nearly to the floor. He nonetheless sported a veritable mane of pepper gray hair atop a chiseled face. His ice-blue eyes matched his daughter's in light and intensity.

"Father, may I present Major Leander Liner."

"An honor, sir," Leander said as he walked over and shook the outstretched hand offered him. He was surprised by the strength of the apparent invalid's grip.

"Major, please be seated."

Leander sat in the chair indicated. Reduced to this level, he could now see a pronounced fall in the covers as they left the edge of the seat and made their way down to the footrest. The man had no legs below the knees.

"Yes, Major, I have lost my legs."

Stammering somewhat, Leander was embarrassed at being found out.

"I am sorry, sir."

"The fortunes of war, Major, as you well know. A degree of paralysis accompanies my handicap, necessitating my being here." John Henry patted the chair, no trace of bitterness or self-pity in his cultivated voice. "Perhaps before she takes her leave, Summer will be kind enough to bring us some cigars. Will you join me, Major?"

Leander fairly leapt at the offer, lit the cigar Summer handed him, and sat back. After a moment he remarked, "Excellent."

"My blend, Major. We have over twenty-five acres in tobacco. But these matters are not what draws you here, is it?"

Grateful for the smoke and the opening, Leander gathered his thoughts and responded, "No, sir, it is not. I know how strange this all must seem to you, but I have fallen in love with your daughter. Of that, there is no question. I, therefore, circumstances notwithstanding, ask your permission and blessing for her hand in marriage."

"Very well. You have been forthright with me, Major. I will respond in kind. I lost my legs in combat serving with your General Lee in Mexico. While there, I too fell in love with a woman, a native, whom I married and brought back to this, our family ancestral home, much to the chagrin of my parents. I say all that to say this, Major: I know what war is and I know what it is to fall in love in time of war. You cannot mix the two without detriment to one or the other or both. You wish to marry my daughter. Very well, I give my consent. But not now, sir, not before this business is finished. When that occurs, and if you survive it, come back and I, *we*, will welcome you into our family."

Leander considered this and after a moment responded, "Fairly spoken, sir, I thank you and will abide by your wishes."

"One more thing, Major. Do not let thoughts of my daughter, your love for her or hers for you, affect your demeanor or actions in conflict. The moment you begin to change your nature to accommodate her or the feelings you hold for her is the moment a bullet will find you out." John Henry fell silent now, smoothing the covers over his stumps, quietly reflecting on another place, another time, another life. "I sense you are a warrior, Major. Stay one, the rest will take care of itself."

Leander again considered what the man had said and again nodded in agreement. There was one other thing he needed to ask.

"Your wife, Summer's mother?"

"Smallpox, two years ago."

Leander stood. "Yes, sir, thank you."

"I hope it will prove to be that it is I who has to thank you, Major. My daughter is everything to me. Good day, Leander."

"Good day, sir."

Leander walked to the door, turned, and looked back at the restricted yet proud figure of John Henry Will. A subtle nod between them conveyed an understanding that transcended words.

He rejoined Summer on the porch and took her hands in his. "With God as my witness, I love you, and when this is over, I will be back for you." He kissed her mouth gently, and in that moment, knew he would remember this moment forever.

She spoke. "With that same God as my witness, I will be here waiting for you." He embraced her again, kissing the open mouth harder, running his hands down until he held the small of her back as she pressed against him. He realized the plain chiffon dress was all she had on as she pushed herself on his hardness. Briefly, lightly, he allowed his callused hands to cup the full, taut roundness of her cheeks. They drew apart at the last manageable moment, looking into each other with the promise of all that lay warm and implied between them.

He mounted up and motioned to Traylor.

"Where will you go now?"

"I don't really know. Looks as if both armies are gathering at a place near here—Gettysburg, I think." They rode off, through fields that seemed somehow more barren now.

Summer stood on the porch and watched Leander ride off until both he and the wagon were nearly out of sight and the waves of heat rising from the dusty road melted with his outline, and then—he was gone. She was leaning against a post, arms crossed over nipples still hardened from their embrace. Her legs were crossed near the knees, the bulk of her weight resting on one leg, the other intermittently tapping a foot on the floor. The moistures of passion denied condensed on the soft black curled hairs surrounding her gender and then, yielding, fell down the inside of her long, brown thighs. Inwardly, she smiled.

Into this reflective, sensual reverie Rose came bursting through the screen door in a fit of feigned indignation. "Summer Will! You gets yourself in this house! I never *seed* such carryin' on in all my born days!"

Still languishing in her memory, Summer looked off toward the horizon. "Rose, I'm gonna marry that man."

"Huh! The way you carryin' on, folks think you was takin' your *honeymoon* right here on dis porch! Never *seed* anythin' like it! Shame on you, Summer Will! Why, I do believe I seed that man git a handful of your posterior right here! Did I *see* that, Summer Will?"

"Two handfuls, Rose, two."

"Lawd, Lawd, protect me! Rose gotta have air!" She fluttered one hand in front of her face. "'*Two* handfuls,' she says. And proud of it! Lawd, Lawd!" Warming to her task now, Rose inquired further, "And did I sees you press your *own* self up agin that man, Summer Will? Did Rose see *that?* Lawd, strike me *blind*!"

"Yes, Rose, you saw it."

"Lawd, Lawd! Rose need a bigger fan! And dat man look to Rose like he was hard aroused. Did Rose see *dat?* Oh, Lawd—don't tell me."

"Rose."

"Yes, 'um?"

"Harder than Chinese arithmetic."

"Help! Lawd! Rose got the vapors!"

"Rose."

"Yes, 'um?"

"Long, hard Chinese arithmetic."

"Sweet Jesus, fetch the smellin' salts! Rose is goin' down!" Only by grabbing the back of a rocking chair did she prevent that seismic catastrophe.

"Rose."

"*No,* Ma'am. No *mo'!* Rose can't take no mo'!"

"Let's go in, Rose."

"Alright, den, but—member, Rose don't want to hear *no mo'*—least wise till she *sittin' down.* Let's go."

Chapter 43

Any war, every war, carries with it the ingredients, the precursors, to either make men into creatures of high moral certitude or depraved fiends. Some are transformed from a menial existence to extraordinary courage and example. Average people find within themselves a purpose and meaning that exalts them to higher planes and standards than they envisioned. It is a profound irony that such things occur in such a place. There are others, however, whose alchemy turns to darker, baser things. The reasons, beliefs, and causes of a great conflict never rise to a noble purpose; they merely engender the course, amoral, mean, low aspects of a sinister, evil nature. They kill, torture, mutilate, and hurt because they can. They do not believe, for belief is somewhere grounded in faith. War is not a means to an end; it is an excuse, an alibi for a malevolency that can find no justification in other times. Every war, each side, all factions, harbor them. Thus it was with Nebo Small. Nebo Small hated Confederates. He detested them with a visceral bile that consumed him as well as any act or thought that might mitigate against his predilection. Reason was an unwelcome visitor to his bias, as useless as trying to account for man's aversion to snakes. No need to discuss it. Just kill them, no matter their breed. They were, after all, snakes. Butternut, gray, venomous reptiles.

He came to this loathing through a catechism fostered in him since childhood by his father, an ordained minister. The Reverend Doctor Hannibal Small was a solitary, bitter, vituperative man who forbade any mention of Nebo's absent mother, a Richmond debutante and the incubus of his father's detestation of everything Southern.

The boy's memory of the vile creature portrayed by his father was a hazy, if contradictory, confluence of soft, luxuriant black hair falling across an engorged brown breast, the faint hint of citrus, and a melodic, sweet, drawn voice cooing lullabies.

It was against this formidable backdrop of maternal memories that the Reverend launched his quite uncivil war to eradicate any vestige of affection between his banished wife and their one child. True to his new religion of fanaticism, Dr. Small was not content to merely destroy any familial bond between the two; he was intent on replacing it with a very real aversion to and repudiation of all she represented. In this undertaking, he was unquestionably successful, for Brevet Captain Nebo Small hated Confederates.

He came to initial rank by the political machinations of his father and rose through the influence of General Butler, whom he served under in New Orleans. Women did not like him, nor did men. He was an obsequious, pallid, duplicitous little man who enjoyed watching dogs fight and men beat women, so long as the man—Small entertained a preference here—was white. The woman could be any color; it didn't matter, so long as she was violated beforehand. Such entertainment was not hard to find in the Crescent City.

Captain Small's chosen field was loosely called intelligence where subterfuge, lying, and larceny were much desired. All these attributes he possessed in abundance, and when coupled with his natural proclivity to be utterly devoid of conscience, they made him a most valuable staff member. He would do any and everything no one else would. Unfortunately, Butler recognized a kindred spirit, and in so doing, also saw a potential liability should Small ever decide to reveal his duties, so the "Beast" promoted Small to Captain in the newly formed Bureau of Military Information and shipped him off to Virginia.

The practitioners of "intelligence" work, in both the North and, in particular, the South, were not held in very high esteem by their comrades. The men—and women—engaging in these activities occupied a questionable arena of conventional military operations. Nevertheless, the dim light of clandestine operations suited Nebo Small and he scoffed when told Lee had said, "Gentlemen don't read each other's mail." Essentially accountable to no one, he had carte blanche to do as he wished, and his most fervent wish was to inflict pain on Confederates, not as a means to an end. It was justification in and of itself. Nebo likened it to putting down a rabid animal. He did have to subscribe to some nominal prohibitions, but these he satisfied by having an inordinate number of prisoners shot while trying to escape, hanging themselves, or simply killing each other. No one cared, no one asked. His own men's aversion to him insured this. So, Brevet Captain Nebo Small was attached in a most ancillary manner and left alone to ply his trade.

"Captain Small, Colonel says you're to take a detail and investigate a family he says is selling provisions to the Rebs."

"Very well, Sergeant, gather the men—you know the ones I want—and saddle my horse."

"Yes, sir."

Small's group made their way at a leisurely pace towards the farm, following direction given them by a Federal sympathizer. Not unlike Leander, Small's first impression of the Will farm was one of awe, but unlike his Confederate counterpart, his reaction was immediately transformed into a revulsion that anything so beautiful could be associated with, not to mention give aid to, the enemy.

Summer met the blue-clad band from the front porch, having been apprised of their arrival by Zeke. Her immediate aversion to the officer leading them was hard to conceal, but she managed, sensing the potential ramifications of his presence.

"Madam, I am Captain Small. It is our understanding that you have been abetting the Confederate forces in rebellion against the lawful government of these United States."

"We have done no such thing, sir, and I would appreciate your leaving now."

"When and how I leave is not in your power to decide, madam. I do not think you appreciate the severity of the charges against you."

"I understand the severity, Captain. I deny them absolutely."

"Did you or did you not provide provisions in the form of foodstuffs to the Rebels?"

"They took the provisions, Captain, we did not provide them."

"A distinction I find irrelevant."

Summer's dander was up now as she made her way down the porch so that she was standing directly in front of Small. "I can give you the facts, "Mr." Small, but not the understanding." This rejoinder brought a twitter from the enlisted men accompanying the Federal Captain, but they soon fell silent under his glare.

"Under the authority vested in me, I find you guilty of collusion with the enemy. Sergeant, burn this house and all out buildings to the ground." The members of the detail simply looked at each other, not believing Small was serious, trying to find some reasoning in the awkward moment. "Sergeant, you and these men are a breath away from having charges leveled against you. Do you wish to be court martialed?" Resigned to their task now, the Sergeant ordered his men to accompany him to the barn. They would begin there and let the Captain take his chances with the fiery proprietress.

John Henry came around the porch corner being pushed by Rose. A shotgun rested across his lap. "Captain, you would be well advised to leave this place now."

"As would you, sir, and this black mammy, before I level it."

Working primarily with just one arm, John Will made to raise his gun. Crying out, "No!", Summer grabbed the barrel and had almost wrestled the weapon from her father's grasp when an explosion rent the air. The force of the 44-caliber slug from Captain Small's Starr revolver drove Will and his chair back against the house wall. The next one slammed him back in the chair, then he fell forward onto the porch. The third round turned him over, exposing two gaping holes in his chest. He had been quite dead after the first shot. Summer stared down at her father in disbelief, then, wielding the long gun like a club, she flew off the porch, swinging at Small. He kicked her full in the face, rendering her unconscious and prostrate on the ground. Rose fell to her knees wailing, looking back and forth at Summer, then her father. Small dismounted, holstered his revolver and went in the front door. He made his way upstairs and methodically began to shatter all the oil lamps, setting their spilled contents ablaze. He repeated his pyrotechnic destruction throughout the first floor and was walking out when he noticed a Confederate Quartermaster receipt lying on a credenza in the hall. He picked it up as the flames gained momentum and read: "Received of John Henry and Summer Will, provisions in the amount of $642 Confederate. Signed, Traylor Crockett, Sergeant on behalf of Leander Liner, Major, CSA." He folded the paper and placed it in his tunic pocket. "I should have shot them all," he murmured.

Rose was verging on hysteria as Small walked past her, then stopped, turned, and slapped her through the face. "Best stop crying, mammy, and get this body off the porch. Unless, of course, you like roast Reb." He laughed at his alliteration and mounted up, signaling the detail to follow him, after spotting smoke plumes issuing from the barn.

Rose drug the limp, lifeless body of her old friend down the steps, grimacing each time his head bounced on a tread. Soon, she had both John Henry and Summer far from the conflagration that was once their home. Oddly, only a few wisps of smoke came from the huge barn and she hurried to investigate. The Union soldiers had merely raked some hay to its center, in front of the doors, and lit it to give the appearance of a real fire. The barn was saved. It was something. She went back to tend Summer. John Henry would no longer need her, and Rose cried tears as big as her heart.

Chapter 44

As July 1st drew to a close, Leander sensed both armies had sustained heavy casualties. He heard through the camp rumor mill that Lee was perplexed by Stuart's absence. If he was indeed off on another grand ride, Leander shared the dismay, for no army could properly function without its eyes. Two of his fellow brigades under Pender, Thomas's and Perrin's, were assigned to Trimble for the next day's engagement.

"Why in God's name we did not commit everything necessary to take that ridge with the cemetery on it is beyond me, Othello. Or, failing that, why did we not then secure that other prominence some eight hundred yards to the east? Culp's Hill, I believe it is. It would have made their possession of the ridge untenable. Ewell seems to me a different man these days."

Othello nodded. "Strange, ain't it? No man who has lost a leg in battle, then who must be strapped to a horse so as to ride into another, can have his bravery questioned, but they say he's no longer aggressive."

"I hear Gordon asked, nay begged, to be allowed to seize it, but was met with silence."

On the 2nd day, Pender's Division was essentially inactive while Longstreet attacked Sickles's Federals with Hood's Division. They swept through a bolder-strewn area called the Devil's Den in fierce hand-to-hand combat and moved on the small prominence of Little Round Top. The Federal 5th Corps was able to repulse the attack. At about the same time, General McLaws attacked through a peach orchard and wheat field. Once again, intense fighting stalled the Confederate advance before they could reach Cemetery Ridge. Anderson assaulted the Union center while Johnson made to take Culps Hill, and Early drove on Cemetery Hill. Most were either driven back by counterattack or managed to hold modest gains. All this cost some ten thousand men on each side.

Lee was determined to force the issue, ruling a flanking maneuver impracticable. For better or worse, Leander agreed. Meade was a good general—it was not as if he would simply stay still and allow himself to be flanked. Nevertheless, it now was rumored that Longstreet had sulled up after urging that Lee interpose himself between Washington and the Union forces. Lee was also keenly aware of the dearth of provisions for his men and animals. He would hit the Union center on Cemetery Ridge while Ewell renewed his assault on Culps Hill. Stuart—present now and remorseful—would move around the Union's right flank to attack the rear. The move against Culps Hill began at dawn, lasted for six hours, and only saw the Confederates able to withdraw back beyond Rock Creek stream. Stuart was met by Union cavalry and the attempt to move against the Federal rear was thwarted. Then came the major offensive. At 1 p.m. some 160 Rebel cannons opened up on the enemy's center. As Leander watched—he was held in reserve—they hammered the Federals for over two hours. He had never before witnessed such a bombardment. And yet, he could not understand why they did not position their artillery so as to enfilade the Union lines instead of the frontal attack now under way. Most of the thousands of shots either fell short or sailed over Union lines. Additionally, those Federal forces aligned on the lower slopes were unscathed. Had they been shooting *down* the enemy's line, something would have been hit. Around 2, the Federals ceased returning fire, leading Confederates to think they had silenced their batteries. One hour later, at 3 p.m., 12,000 Confederate soldiers began to make their way across the open fields towards Union lines. When the gray horde reached the Emmitsburg Road, the silent Union batteries opened on them, inflicting heavy casualties. Still they came on. Leander then saw a most distressing sight. A fence seemed to hold up the advance, and worse, funneled the infantrymen towards an opening, where the Union cannon and rifle simply slaughtered his comrades. Still they came on, and some reached Union lines but—but what—Leander speculated—there was no second wave, no reinforcement, no reserve sent forward. It was not war, it was murder. The attack failed.

The next night, July 4th, Lee began to retreat towards Virginia. He accepted, nay, claimed responsibility, but Leander could not but wonder if Longstreet had followed the letter and spirit of his orders. Gettysburg cost the Confederates some 28,000 casualties. The Union count was nigh on 23,000.

Leander wanted desperately to stop off and see Summer, but there was too much to do. Their rear guard fought off an ineffectual pursuit. And the wounded, so many wounded, needed attention. Additionally, a real question existed as to whether or not they would be able to recross rain-swollen rivers in order to reach the relative safety of Virginia. Summer would have to wait, and that realization pained Leander more than he ever imagined.

Letters Home

July 5, 1863

dear mama,
I am good but hurt sum. In the fight yesturday a shell blowed up near me and my haid was cut open and my ear hung loose. I was out cold fer a spell. When I come to, I made my way to the house wher they was fixin up us that was hurt. The doc took one swipe and off come my ear. He sewed up my haid then cause I was not so bad I had to help with the rest. Mama it was awful. I went out and sat up agin the house and fell to sleep. When I woke up they was throwin arms and laigs and parts out the window next to me they had cut off. Oh mama this fightin is bad. Out come a hand then a leg then a foot in a boot then a hole arm. They had to cut them off so the man what had them could live on. Some do some die. The hollerin and screamin and moanin is awful to. They do not have nothin to give them to help the pain. Lots died out whur I was hit. They could not move and cried for water or a loved one. The shells put the woods on fire and hit got them poor men. Oh to here them hollar. Kill me they say kill me. We found them like they was still trying to hollar. Anyway like I said they put me to work toteing off all them parts they cut off. First we used a wheelbarrow and then a wagon. Sum dug a pit then we filled it up. We took the rings and shoos and such and giv them back in case they made it. I never would have said I would say this but I long to go back to fightin. Tell everybody I say hay.
    Your son,
    Caleb

Chapter 45

The python's girth was the equal of a man's leg. The constrictions slowly banished the last molecule of air from Leander's body. As they rolled in their dance of death, he wondered, in a manner that was detached, as if he were witnessing someone else grappling with the serpent, whether their inexorable progress towards deep water meant he would die of suffocation or drowning.

"Leander, Leander, wake up, you're having another one of those dreams." He was lifted from his somnolent quagmire of terror by hands on his shoulders and imploring words in his ear. He awoke and looked up with relief into Othello's concerned face. Othello handed him his canteen.

"Let's join the others by the fire."

"I don't know."

"I hear the professors back." They both laughed.

"OK, let's go."

The "professor" was a 29-year-old scholar from Mississippi who reportedly had graduated from Harvard, studied at the Sorbonne, Heidelberg, and Glasgow. His occasional visits were the cause of great rejoicing around the evening's campfires, for the men loved to listen to him expound, and they were never disappointed.

As Leander and Othello sat beside Traylor, a jug came their way, and they all drank, Othello from a cup so as not to offend anyone. The professor sometimes regaled them with his interpretations on the great events of history, but this night he embarked on his vision of what the future might hold. To think about or talk about anything but the moment was a communal blessing to soldiers, and he held their rapt attention.

"Gentlemen, if I may be so bold as to beseech you for a taste of that jug going around, I would be most grateful." The jug was forthcoming. "Excellent." It did not escape the attention of the professor's disciples that he stood the jug beside him after drinking and a howl of protest went up to pass it on.

"Certainly, gentlemen, I was distracted."

Someone called out from the ranks, "By what, perfessor?" This mild incentive was usually adequate to set him off on an exposition.

"By a wonderful vision of man in flight, gentlemen, a glorious picture of man aloft."

Hoots and catcalls followed.

"No, I am serious. It is my considered opinion that man, within the next 100 years, will fly."

"Hell, perfessor, I've see'd 'em fly already. I saw a fella catch a solid round last week, and he flew four ways from Sunday." It is the privilege and purview of soldiers to laugh at such things, and they did.

"No, sir, I mean of his own volition, in a craft designed for the purpose."

"Well, don't them Yanks fly already in them damn balloons they got to spy on us?"

"That, sir, is mere ascension, employing gas."

"As much gas as this army has, looks like we could all fly." With that wry observation a calliope of farts issued from around the circle, accompanied by a chorus of laughter.

"Off key but well modulated," the professor intoned, "but no, I mean to say some sort of powered flight."

"Now 'zactly what would this contraption look like, professor?"

"That I do not know, sir, but I have the rudiments of its construction in mind. I think flapping will get us nowhere, but a foil or wing is essential. It must be powered by something, perhaps a steam engine. The drive will probably be a propeller of sorts, much like those that drive ships, except in this instance, the medium through which it moves will be air instead of water."

Silence settled over the group as they grappled with this consternation.

Having enticed the audience thus far, the professor let loose with his real brain-buster. "Further, gentlemen, it is my contention that, using the same forces inherent in hurling a cannon ball, man will, within that same approximate time frame, someday send a craft there." In a most theatrical manner he raised his arm, and pointed to the yellow moon, made full just the night before. All heads turned upwards following the path indicated. The brief, ensuing, almost reverent silence was then shattered by raucous laughter of men rolling on the ground, slapping each other, howling and pointing at the moon.

As the laughter and crying died down, one simple-minded private from Florida rose to his feet while shaking his head and addressed the professor as if talking to a child.

"Now, perfessor, I've heard a lost of bullshit in my day, but this beats all. In case you missed it there is one reason, plain and true, that you can't go sending no craft to the moon, even if all them other things you said was so."

"And what might that be, my friend?"

"Well hell, professor, it ain't even there all the time."

A stunned silence engulfed the group as they pondered this common-sense reproach to all the professor's prognostications. Satisfied they had refuted his every argument, the men made their respective ways back to their campsites. This, of course, after yet another pull on the jug.

Chapter 46

The spirits of the 16th, as well as the rest of the Army of Northern Virginia, were bolstered to a nearly unprecedented degree as the new Union Commander, Grant, continuing his inexorable movement towards Richmond, clashed with Lee at the vital crossroads of Cold Harbor. Three days of inconclusive clashes prompted Grant to launch a massive frontal assault, where, in a mere thirty minutes, the Union forces suffered over seven thousand casualties. Confederate losses were barely fifteen hundred. Lee had won a major victory. And yet, still the blue clad masses pushed south towards the James River. Finding the approaches to Richmond well defended, Grant quickly shifted his forces south of the river and set his sights on Petersburg.

On the 15th of June '64, Leander was attempting to rally his men in an engagement near Piedmont, Virginia. The Federals with heavy artillery support attacked a gap in their line. General Imboden was prevented from lending support to General "Grumble" Jones's troops by Union cavalry. Jones's death precipitated the disintegration of the Confederate line and it was into this breech that Leander stepped. He had shifted his sword to his left hand, waving the men on, when a partially spent cannonball struck his upraised arm behind and just above its elbow. The blow spun him around, and when he was righted, he found himself possessed of an odd anatomical arrangement as he attempted to raise the sword again. From his shoulder to just near his elbow, his arm pointed toward the sky as he intended. The remainder of the appendage, however, hung limply at an acute angle straight towards the ground, much as a plumb bob would. Leander examined his misshapen arm and noticed his unresponsive hand still clutched the sword. Touching the metal ever so lightly, he watched with detached wonder as both arm and weapon swung through a small proscribed arch, like a pendulum set in motion. He marveled at this, and then the pain hit, and he collapsed in the opening throes of shock.

Leander's commander, Colonel Stowe, found him, prostrate on the ground, his left arm extended at an obscene angle. In the maelstrom accompanying battle, the Colonel made a decision to leave Leander where he found him, reasoning the medical care he would receive by the Union forces outweighed any other considerations. But first, he resolved to deal with the rapidly swelling and distended broken arm. He secured a bandana tightly around the upper arm in hopes it would staunch the flow of blood from what he was resolved to do next. He palpated the broken juncture, feeling nothing but soft tissue. He lifted the arm and slid a shattered fence post under it. Drawing his sword, he brought it down decisively on the break, severing the damaged arm. He whispered a quick benediction for his beloved major and went off to gather the depleted fragments of his command.

Union soldiers on burial detail found Leander the next morning. Because of his rank, they notified their commander, who had the officer removed to an aide station in a nearby farmhouse. The care he received there saved his life. Though still not ambulatory, Leander was carted off to another house two nights later on order of a Captain Small for purposes of interrogation. Leander was lucid but weak. He thanked his captors for their kindness as they deposited him in a chair placed in the center of what had been the parlor in the now abandoned dwelling. A solitary lamp sat on the floor illuminating the interior. Small entered through one of two doors in the room and dismissed the men, saying he had his own troops outside. In fact, he was alone, as he preferred. He walked around his prey slowly, touching him first here, then there with his riding crop. A small, unobtrusive pressure against the rebel's stump brought a wince of pain to the prisoner and a fleeting smile to Small. A few maggots, loosened by the action, fell to the floor.

"So, Major, I see you have company. Fitting, if I may say so. Perhaps I should simply let them devour your traitorous carcass and be done with it." Above the stench of his half arm, Leander sensed something much more odoriferous in the room.

"What do you want?"

"Why, information, Major, information. As any good intelligence officer would." Leander suddenly felt very tired, overcome.

"What possible information could I have that would interest the Union army? We both know this war is over, it's just a matter of time."

"Indeed, Major, just a matter of time. No, my interests are not so grand as to warrant the attention of high command. I just wanted you to explain this." He pulled the quartermaster's receipt from his pocket and dangled it in front of Leander's face. For a moment, he could not make out the writing nor grasp the importance of so mundane a piece of paper. Then he read "John and Summer Will." He gathered himself and lunged for Small, but his interrogator sidestepped as Leander plunged to the floor in a writhing mass of pain, anger, and confusion. Drawing his knees up to his chest, he wrapped his good arm around his legs in an abbreviated fetal position. Nodding his head in small repetitious movements, he asked, "Why, why?"

"My dear Major, I confess to being somewhat taken aback by your reaction. After all, these people are, or were, mere traitors. Why would their fate so concern you?" Small paced in circles around the prostrate form on the floor, occasionally nudging Leander's stump in order to evoke a groan. "Unless, of course, the lovely Miss Will plays a larger role in this drama than I thought. Is that it, Major? Do you covet the sensual pleasures of the fair maiden? Perhaps you have already availed yourself of them? Aye? Did you couple with the traitorous bitch, Major? Was it good? Well, it is my unfortunate duty to inform you that in the course of my duties, it became necessary to execute her noble father and, let me see if I can recall what it was that happened to your slut. Uhh, yes, I, or should I say my men and I, left her face down in the dirt. She *was* good Major, but of course you know that." Leander made to grab Small's leg but his strength was inadequate to the task, and he received a kick in his midriff for his exertion. Leander simply moaned, "Why? Why?"

"Why? Why indeed, my dear Major. Actually it's very simple and elegant if I may say so myself. With your help, I intend to prove the Wills traitors. Having done that, I have made arrangements after the war, which you have so presciently foretold as nearly over, to obtain their magnificent estate for a pittance. Brilliant, aye? I confess that initially I thought I had made an emotional, if not tactical blunder when I had burned the house down. However, God smiles on the righteous, does he not, Major? It turns out that little fire proved my legitimacy when negotiating for the property. Why, I asked them, would I burn something if I had designs on it? Now, all I need is your signature on this document admitting complicity on their part, and I promise you a quick ending. If not, well then, I do have my ways, and as you can see, nothing on this earth can stop me, or save you."

"Can too."

The voice came gently out of the darkness surrounding the lantern. Leander thought he heard something, but could not make it out nor did he care to. Nebo Small thought it an aberration, the wind, the house creaking, or an animal calling. He looked up towards the ceiling and implored the disembodied voice falling through the musty, dank air, "What?"

"Stops you and saves him."

Again the voice came, but with direction this time. Small whirled towards the sound, drawing his revolver as he turned. The last thing he remembered of this place was an enormous calloused fist, tightly drawn fingers coming out of the night, traveling through darkness, ink into light, yes, that was it; the fist was dark too, the fingers as large as some wrists, coming towards his face very fast, until his whole vision was consumed by it. Then, light, shattered light and pain, and again, blackness, nothing. He knew, on some level, he had watched his own death.

Sycamore picked Leander up, cradled him against his massive chest, and carried him out into the breaking dawn and his waiting wagon parked over on a small rise. He laid him in the back and covered his spasmed shaking with blankets. Before setting off, he lifted the covers and picked a single maggot off Leander's bloody stump. "Be rights back, Boss." He then turned, made his way over the rise, and re-entered the house. He walked over to Small and gazed down at the crumpled mass that was his body. Then he dropped his pale wiggling companion onto the jellied mess of blood, bone, and flesh that had been Captain Nebo Small's face. He wheeled and left.

After mounting the creaking, protesting wagon, he took his accustomed place on the well-worn seat. He expertly took up the reins, set loose the brakes, and turned to check on Leander. His grateful, sick, and somewhat confused patient met his gaze with a quizzical look.

"Dust to dust, boss, dust to dust."

Letters Home

June 15, 1864

Dear Fokes,
I ain't ashamed a bit to say it, I am gonna run. I cannot take no more of this. Today I saw a cannon ball pass thru 4 horses standing side by side. Sum times I think I can handle the killin and I do when it is men. They begun this thing but oh god the animals. They are laid ever which way following a battle fightin to get up with no legs and there guts hangin out. One kep steppin on his own insides trailin after him. They gets blown to bits and it's a mercy if anyone shoots um. We have been ordered not to waste bullets on um. Many of us that can cuts there throats. I don't think I can do this any longer. I believe I will skedaddle the next chance I gets. Many more are doin it to. Please don't think me a coward or shirker. I killed many a man but see no purpose in any of this anymore. I want only to sit at home and watch the sun go down and listen to the whippoorwill lik I used to.
  Your son,
  Elum

Chapter 47

Othello had, as was his custom, followed discreetly behind Leander's regiment as they made their way towards the hamlet of Piedmont. He did so with the full knowledge of everyone in that regiment, except the major from Western North Carolina. The men had understood why he did it and swore themselves to secrecy.

In the skirmish that followed, Othello had hidden himself in an abandoned corncrib awaiting the outcome. While there, he had carefully sifted through the debris, gleaning several handfuls of kernels for their supper that night. Having learned long ago, as all men accustomed to battle do, to sleep through the ruckus, he was not surprised to find it near dusk when he awoke and all was quiet. As he rose to leave, he heard voices behind him, Yankee accents. He burrowed under the dry shucks and froze. The voices came nearer, stopped, and the men carrying them shook the boards lining the crib and struck them with the butts of their guns.

"Come out of there, Johnny Reb!"

For a terrifying moment, Othello thought they had seen him but then—laughter. They moved off. Unfortunately, they only went a short distance before settling down. Within an hour, a whole company had joined them, and all made camp. After dark, one young soldier—he couldn't have been much over fifteen—negotiating his way by moonlight, came back to the crib and actually tore some boards off for firewood. When he left, Othello resolved to move and did. He retraced his steps towards where he assumed the Federals strength lay, but for the moment he judged it safer.

Morning broke with light rain and wind, but it remained warm, thank God, for he had no coat or poncho. The Union troops had broken camp, buried their dead, and moved on, ominously south. Othello tried to place the date and thought it around the middle of June. Two young Negro boys, out scavenging, told him of the fight that had taken place there and pointed out the way taken by the butternut and gray after losing it. They also pointed out all the graves left behind. Othello considered it, but did not have the heart or time—besides, that was a good way to get shot, robbing graves.

He followed in the direction the boys had indicated, anxious to get back to camp with the evidence for his absence in his pocket. He walked along a footpath, paralleling the road, alert for Federal forces. A dull glint amongst the grasses drew his attention and he knelt to investigate. Bile rose in his throat as he recognized the initials LL on the blade followed by 16th North Carolina Infantry. He remembered how touched Leander had been when the men who presented it to him explained how they did not have enough money to spell out infantry and had not put any rank on it because they were sure Leander would be a general someday. He grasped the blade and pulled it free of the undergrowth. He fell back, hurling the blade from him as first a hand, then an arm followed it out.

"Oh, God! Oh, God!" Minutes passed in confusion, anger, guilt, and sadness. He gathered himself and crawled back. He took a stick and turned the arm over. *There!* The wrist bore no hourglass birthmark, as did Leander's! And then he knew. He knew the awful truth and his body revolted and he puked and he sobbed and he moaned and his whole self shook with pain and remorse. It was the left hand attached to the sword. Leander was dead.

Later, he did not know how much later, he roused himself and went about the onerous task he knew he must perform. Although he essentially had to break the fingers, he freed the sword from the disembodied hand that had so often clasped his. Next, he dug a hole—grave—with the sword itself, laid Leander's arm in it and covered it over. He removed his dirty, misshapen slouch hat and prayed, "Now cracks a noble heart. Good night, sweet prince, and flights of angels sing thee to thy rest."

He rose, wrapped the sword in a piece of cloth discarded by the Union campers, and moved off south, towards their last camp.

Chapter 48

Sycamore drew the wagon into an overhang of willows and listened—water. This would make a good camp—secluded and quiet. He urged the mule on, deeper into the canopy until they emerged in a clearing dissected by a brook. He unharnessed the weary animal and staked him in the middle of some clover, close by running water. Next he built a fire, hung a pot over it, and filled it half full with water. He then unwrapped a possum he had shot and gutted that morning. With practiced hands, he severed the head, cut the legs, and skinned it. He ran a peeled stick through it lengthwise and suspended the carcass over the fire between two other sticks he had cut for that purpose.

Having prepared camp, Sycamore now set about to comfort his companion and began helping Leander from the wagon and placing him by the fire. Gently, he began to cut the crusty sleeve from Leander's amputated arm.

"Sycamore, how in God's name did you come to be there?"

"Later, Boss. Rights now I gots to contend wid dis." Looking down at his stump, Leander saw the maggots crawling around it, but many were falling off of their own volition.

"Oh God, Sycamore, get those things off me!"

"Dey done done der job, boss, eatin' dat dead meat. I gets 'um off now." Sycamore poured some liquid out of a small dark bottle into the heart of the wound.

"What's that?" Leander asked, wincing from the pain.

"Ni-trick acid, boss. It help."

"You are a wonderment, Sycamore Pin Oak. Show up out of nowhere carrying medicine. Are you an angel?" Leander was serious.

So was Sycamore. "No, Boss, but what go 'round, come 'round. Dat in da Good Book—if it ain't, hit oughd'a be."

"How did you find me?"

"Likes I said, Boss, later ons. Dat arm need tendin' now." He turned their meal, and after pouring off some of the now boiling water, dropped coffee grounds into what remained, then cleaned the wound with cloth and water and set about removing the sutures.

"I don't understand—why are you doing that?"

"Well, Boss, I answers bofe your questions. I been makin' my way as a teamster, coming south, always south. Got tied up wid the medical folk hauling stuff, helpin' out. Learns a lot. For x-ample, done find out dis old horsehair tie da South use better den dem fancy silk 'uns dey employ. Don't know why, jus is." As was the custom, Sycamore then dropped a bundle of unwrapped sutures into the boiling water he had drawn off, unknowingly answering his own question. Then with a dexterity that belied hands so large, he finished taking out the remaining sutures in his patient's arm. The bleeding was minimal. "Dis may sting," he forewarned Leander as he poured moonshine from an earthen jug over the wound. "Maybe better git a little of dat *in* you, to attack da sickness from dat side." Leander laughed—God that felt good—and took a long pull from the jug. God, that felt good too.

"Doc, don't you reckon you better have a pull? Only seems fair."

"Fair is fair." Sycamore intoned as he put the mouth of the jug to his lips and worked his Adam's apple up and down for three or four good swallows. "I like dis doctorin' a hole lots more dan drivin' dem mules." They both laughed. Good medicine.

Sycamore once again poured the nitric acid into the wound after he had reapplied the new sutures. Next, he bound up the stub with clean cloth.

"Der now."

"Thank you."

"Welcome, let's eat." They devoured the possum, drained the coffee, and then Sycamore cut them each a plug and they sat back to chew. "Well, Boss, I tooks dat money you give me and went saw dem folks. Dey was most oblidgin'. Dey gots my chillren bought off and we headed north. Settled in Massachusetts. Sycamore's little girl babies all good. I tell dem no mo man gonna whip der daddy. But Sycamore owe a debt and gots to pay it, so I comes. Sycamore ain't partial to owin' no man. Didn't know he'd find you in dis fix."

" But how did you find me in all this mess?"

"I knowed your outfit, just took time and askin'. Den, I jus list'n. Sycamore hear things other folks don't. Den, I jus' follow my compass, da one inside me, and dare you is, being hauled off by dat fella what's empty inside like a haint. Now I feels I is paid up."

"Well, I think you've done that, and more."

"Your call, Boss."

"I just did."

They chewed and spat and looked into the embers.

Sycamore spoke, "Dat fella back dare—what wrong wid him?"

"I don't know, just mean, I guess."

"Mean don't cover him. Sumthin' wrong wid dat boy's soul."

"Yes, I guess it is—was."

"Was is right, da rest 'tween him and his maker."

"Sycamore, you heard the folks he mentioned, the Wills?"

"Yea, I heard."

"Well, you see, the girl—the woman—I—have no right to ask, but she and I—and you've paid any debt you might have owed, and now, I owe you. But I have to know."

"I knows. I checks up on it."

"Thank you. The mail is so unreliable, and I must get back to my regiment. If you can, I would yet again be indebted to you."

"I do it. No needs to tell me. I hear in your words how you feels in your heart."

"I don't doubt that, Sycamore; you're a wise man."

"But travelin' north 'stead of east, I reckon." They both laughed at the wisdom and wit of the big man. Again Sycamore spoke first. "How 'bout another pull, den we rest?"

"Doctor's orders?"

"Pre-scribed."

"Pass the jug of—ahh—medicine."

"Here 'tis."

"Sycamore, I've got some things to sort out and think about. How about me taking the first watch? All I have to do is sit here—and I'll wake you for your turn."

"Fine with me, Boss. Sycamore frazzled."

"Good. Rest well, and, Sycamore, thank you again."

"Hush."

"Yes, sir."

The big man awoke at dawn to the irritating call of a blue jay.

"Boss, how comes you don't wake me?"

"I was skeered to. God, what a snore! No matter. I needed the time and you needed the sleep."

Stretching his massive arms and rolling his log of a neck around on shoulders so broad his children sat on them as if they were park benches, Sycamore agreed. "I do feels good. Thank you, Boss. Snored, huh?"

"I was afraid Grant might hear it."

"Grant! You funny, Boss. Grant way over yonder."

They set out, debts squared.

As they were leaving, Sycamore handed Leander a dark blue bottle from under the wagon seat. "Riding in de back of dis wagon gonna be tough on dat arm. Drink dis. Put you out, no problem." Leander eyed the bottle with some suspicion.

"What is it?"

"Laudanum."

"I think I can make it."

"Your call, Boss, but you need to sleep, too. Let me know if you change your outlook." They had not traveled over one hour when the heat and the bumps and the flies changed Leander's outlook.

"Sycamore—"

"Here tis, Boss. You rest." Leander downed the contents and within ten minutes was fast asleep.

Chapter 49

Othello was approaching a crossroads when he saw a dust trail and the wagon that was its source coming from the west. Their progress would place them at the intersection about the same time. Always wary in these situations, he eyed the wagon and its driver very carefully, intending to cut across field if necessary. He did not relish explaining his possession of a Confederate officer's sword to some redneck. As the wagon slowly drew closer, he remarked to himself, "That's the biggest hunk of black man I've seen since—" Could it be? How many Negroes were that size? He continued to approach with caution until the driver came into view.

"Sycamore Pin Oak, is that you?"

The driver pulled on the reins, called, "Whoa, mule," and eyed Othello.

"Othello! I be damned, here you is, too! How is you, boy?"

"Sycamore, it sure is good to see you! Can I hitch a ride?"

"Shor can, but keeps your voice down, Leander's asleep."

Othello stopped in his tracks as he made to mount the wagon, and then stepped back, looking up at the big black man.

"Sycamore, it is good to see you, but that ain't funny. I just buried his arm and calling it 'sleep' don't help." Now Sycamore was confused and somewhat upset.

"What you want me to call it?"

"Dead, Sycamore, dead. You don't have to employ a euphemism." Now the giant was more upset than confused and said so.

"Now, you listens. I ain't gonna hire on no u-nism, whatever dat is, but Sycamore Pin Oak know sleeping from dying and dat man in da back of dis wagon, Leander Liner, is asleep." Othello saw that he was serious and rushed the wagon, jumped on the wheel and climbed up. There—there was Leander, minus an arm, but asleep, drool running from the side of his mouth. Othello broke down and began sobbing.

Sycamore understood now. He had thought Leander was dead. No wonder he was so testy. "I is sorry, I thought you knowed."

"No, but this—this is wonderful."

"Is, ain't it? I lets him tell you when he comes to. Filled him with Laudanum. Come on, let's git."

"Yes, lets." Othello climbed over onto the seat besides Sycamore, took one more look back at Leander, let out a monumental sigh and then sized up his driver.

"Sycamore. Sometimes, someways. somethings are larger than life. I reckon you're one of 'um." The big man swelled with pride and shook the reins.

"Come up, Sally, come up."

With the help of several local farmers, Sycamore and Leander were able to find the decimated and struggling army of North Virginia while avoiding the Union forces. Nevertheless, it surprised Leander that Grant had chosen to bypass Richmond, flank Lee, and lay siege to Petersburg, south of the capital city. Upon reflection, though, Leander saw the reasoning in it. Petersburg was the last remaining rail juncture in the state, linking Richmond and Lee's army with the Deep South through four different lines. Lay seize here and sever all the Confederate lifelines. It was just a matter of time. It was also just a matter of duty for the approximately 100,000 men with Leander who faced almost one million Federals. Leander was placed on indefinite sick leave while some of the 16th were temporarily assigned to Thomas's Legion, joining General Jubal Early in his Valley Campaign.

The reunion between Traylor and Sycamore was a sight to behold. They shouted and danced around, raining blows down on each other that would fell lesser men. They decided a celebration was in order and were not the least dismayed when told that food for the banquet table would consist of stale crackers infested with weevils.

"You boys don't know where to look," Traylor informed them. "Me and this little fella here will be back by dark with the goods."

"Ah, Boss, where do we gonna look?" Sycamore inquired as they made preparations to leave.

"Underwater, Sycamore, underwater."

Following Crockett's lead, the pair made for a pond two or so miles off. En route, Traylor explained his reasoning.

"You see, Sycamore, they was fightin' 'round that pond last week. There's a few dead animals in the water, but I'm guessin' that'll be just the thing for what we want."

"I gots you now, Boss, catfish and turtles."

"Exactly."

When they arrived, their conjecture proved accurate, as they could see one of the objects of their quest feeding on a half submerged and partially decomposed horse that was still tied to a broken caisson. Snapping turtles, at least fifteen of them, were gorging themselves. The two men waded into the gruesome frenzy, and carefully avoiding the dangerous jaws, grasped the stinking, muddy prehistoric beasts by first the front of their shell and then the back, throwing them to shore. Next, one would hold a stick out towards the angry reptilians causing them to lunge and grasp the end in their powerful mouths. Now, anyone who's ever had any dealings with a snapping turtle knows that once they grab hold of something, Gabriel himself could not get them to let loose. Using this attribute against their quarry, the stick holder would pull, forcing the head up and out from under the carapace. The other partner would then slip a chopping block under the outstretched scaly neck and bring a hatchet down, decapitating the animal. Having killed seven or eight of them, the hunters next turned their attention to their other prey—catfish.

"We gonna hook 'em or what, Boss?"

"Or what, Sycamore? We ain't got the hooks or the time to catch 'em regular, so...."

"So we gonna go in and root 'um out of dose banks?"

"Exactly—you done this before?"

"Po folks got po ways, Boss."

Traylor smiled. "Let's go. I brought us a glove."

"Good, dat make it a whole lot easier and cuts way down on da' slime."

The two men slipped on the big cavalry gloves Traylor had gotten and stepped easily into the pond so as not to muddy the waters any more than necessary. They walked over to a portion of the pond fronted by a bank, then submerged and began probing holes with their gloved hand. When they felt or saw movement they would simply grab the fish by its mouth and haul it out. Soon they had harvested several fish weighing from five to twenty pounds. They skinned and gutted the fish, then wrapped them in wet cloth for the trip back. Their harvest was such that they elected to build a makeshift sled of sorts, stretching a blanket between the skids to hold their bounty, and then they dragged their larder back to camp.

Their reception by Company L was tumultuous. The men spent as much time fending off other members of the 16th as they did jostling each other to partake of their feast. They promoted Traylor to the rank of General, and since Sycamore wasn't in the ranks, they just made him Emperor since President was taken. The meal and the music and the singing were a welcome diversion from the drudgery and death to which they were accustomed.

Chapter 50

With directions and a letter of introduction from Leander, Sycamore set out the next morning for Pennsylvania to ascertain the well being of Summer Will. Othello began nursing the one-armed Major back to health in the impoverished environment in which they found themselves. Fortunately, the ministrations of Sycamore and the medicine he left behind served to stem any further infections, and the stump grew healthy. In an orchestrated collusion, Sycamore and Othello had agreed to hide the fact that medicines remained, knowing Leander would insist it be given to others. Othello covered their conspiracy by simply announcing that the potion he was putting on was his own concoction. Simply stated, Othello figured Leander was as warranted a recipient as anyone else might be.

The trip north was relatively uneventful for Sycamore; the few inquiries raised were effectively dealt with by producing his Teamsters papers. Besides, after sizing him up, not many chose to interrogate Mr. Pin Oak at any length.

A week later, Sally pulled the wagon over the hill fronting the Will property at her accustomed measured gate: a reliable, consistent one that was deceptive in the distance covered. Sycamore noticed the charred remnants of a house outlined by four standing brick chimneys. Knowing that Small had done this made knowing what he had done to Small that much more palatable. He made for the huge barn and the human activity he saw there. As he approached, the people scurried inside. He thought he detected three or four Negroes and one white woman.

Reining up in front of the main door he heard a voice call from within, "Who are you and what do you want?"

"Sycamore Pin Oak, and I wants to give you dis here letter from Leander Liner to Miss Summer Will." A woman came tearing out of the barn holding a shotgun in one hand.

"I am Summer Will, Mr. Pin Oak. Please forgive our lack of cordiality. We are wary of strangers here now."

"I understands da nature of dat feeling, but you can rest easy 'bout da source of dis un'." Summer's look reflected her perplexed musing as to the meaning of the big man's words but she hazarded a guess.

"You know of Mr. Small?"

"I know he dealin' wid his maker, if his maker elect to deal wid him."

"God forgive me, sir, but I find that news heartening. Did you say you had correspondence from Leander?"

"No, I gots a letter, doe. Here 'tis." Sycamore handed her the paper, simply folded, no envelope.

It was all Summer could do not to open it and read it on the spot, but her breeding and manners asserted themselves. "Mr. Pin Oak, will you join us for some tea and biscuits?"

"Yes, 'um, I is partial to eatin'."

"Please come down. Rose, will you see to some refreshments for our guest? Zeke, please take Mr. Pin Oak's mule and give it some food and water." Rose came waddling out of the barn wiping her hands on her apron and smoothing her hair into place.

"Come on down off der, big un'."

"Yes 'um," Sycamore responded as he smiled and jumped down, beating the dirt off his clothes.

"Never mind dat. Dirt never hurt nobody. Come on in here." She turned and walked back into the barn, looking coyly over her shoulder as she did so.

Summer took the letter to a log bench and began to read:

> *My Dearest Summer,*
>
> *The outsized man bearing this letter is Sycamore Pin Oak, a friend, and it is no exaggeration to say, a savior. We had a run-in with Captain Small, who let it be known he had shot your father and implied that he—how do I say this—violated you. Whatever the truth, I want you to know it does not matter to me. I just need to know that you are okay. As to me, I fear that when they sound the next "call to arms," I will not respond as I once did. I have lost my left arm, but otherwise am fine. Please respond through Sycamore. I will come to you as soon as this thing is over.*
>
> *Your Loving,*
> *Leander*

Summer sighed, "An arm—what is that?" She fetched pencil and package paper from the barn and composed her response, folded it, and went in to Sycamore.

"I would be most grateful if you would take this to Major Liner, Mr. Pin Oak."

"My pleasure."

"Now tell us of your meeting and all that transpired. Please, leave nothing out."

And so, for the next hour or so, Sycamore regaled his attentive audience with the history of he and Leander's relationship, ending at the present day.

"Fascinating. Leander is indeed fortunate to have you for a friend, Mr. Pin Oak."

"Calls me Sycamore, and I is glad to have him."

Rose chimed in now that the formalities were over. "Is you a married man, Mr. Pin Oak?"

"Rose! What a presumptuous question! Mr. Pin Oak's—Sycamore's—marital status is none of our concern."

"Huh, maybe none of yours, but a lot of mine. Well, is you or ain't you?"

"Widowed, consumption took my wife last year."

"I is sorry! Terrible thing to lose a loved one. Real good thing to find another one." Rose looked closely at their big guest to see if her observation had registered. It had.

Summer tried to steer the conversation to more provincial waters. "Do you have a family, Sycamore?"

"Yes, 'um, three girl babies. Oldest—dat be Mariposa, she sixteen. Dahlia, seven, and Peony, five. Dem my babies."

"What beautiful names."

"Dey is beautiful girl babies."

"Dem babies needs a mama, you axe me," Rose intoned.

"Rose, please."

"Please, nutin', dat's de troof."

"It shore would be a help to der daddy," Sycamore observed.

"See der, what I say?"

"Alright, Rose, alright. Sycamore, you rest here tonight before heading back, and thank you, thank you so much for coming."

"My pleasure, and I reckon I might be coming back," he said as he glanced at Rose, who beamed.

Chapter 51

It was April of '64, and the Siege of Petersburg and all its attendant deprivations had gone on for nearly ten months now, the only bright spot for Leander being his improved health and the positive news from Summer, brought by Sycamore, who had since returned to Massachusetts. Leander had been given permission to return home for recuperation but chose instead to stay with his men, a fact which endeared him even more to them. On the 2nd, the Federal VI Corps broke A.P. Hill's lines, and the General was killed in the assault. A despondent Leander broke the news to Othello. "Poor Lee. First Jackson, then Stuart, now Hill. How does he continue? I'm told that when given news of Hill's death he said, 'He is at rest now, and we who are left are the ones to suffer.' That man carries such burdens and responsibilities, yet he perseveres. No wonder these men love him so. I fear, my friend, that we must break out of this quagmire if we are to have a chance."

Sure enough, orders came down to move west in hopes of them turning south to join forces with Johnston in North Carolina. It was not to be. Their food stores were essentially nonexistent, and the Union troops had captured the main Confederate supply train near Painesville on the 5th. This not only deprived Lee of vital ammunition, but also severed one of his escape routes. As the exhausted and starving Rebels drew close to Salyers Creek on April 6th, the Federals attacked. Despite desperate fighting, Lee lost 8,000 of his army. Yet another, and the last, supply train was captured at Appomattox Station on the 8th, Black Thursday. This, when combined with General Gordon's assertion that he had fought his corps to a frazzle, led Lee to say, "Then there is nothing left for me to do but go and see General Grant, and I would rather die a thousand deaths."

Leander, Traylor, and Othello sat on the ground amid an army in shock, disbelief, and depression. The word had come down that surrender negotiations were under way. "We are at the end of a dream, gentleman, an experiment that failed. I wonder how history will judge us."

"Harshly, Leander," Traylor said, "simply because the victors write the judgement."

"I suppose it may have been foolish anyway. To bring a group espousing states' rights together and try to form a central government may well have been folly from the outset."

"We did our duty as we saw it. No man can do more."

"This will of course end slavery, and I for one am damn glad." Othello and Traylor nodded in quiet agreement. "I don't, as I have said, know how we will be judged by history, but I will tell you this—I heard Alexander urged Lee to conduct guerilla warfare instead of surrendering. To his credit, Lee dismissed the notion. That simple decision portends well for our country."

"Our country?"

"Our country. Now we will see what Grant offers."

"Old 'unconditional'?"

"I don't believe he will do that. The thing now is to heal, not divide us further. I hear Lincoln told him to 'let us up easy.' That too portends well."

The next day, Friday, April 9th, Lee signed the terms of surrender, and word of it preceded him as he made his way back to his headquarters around sunset. It was a sight Leander and anyone else who witnessed it would never forget. Word of his approach ran before him, and men rushed to the road. As he approached, they tried to cheer, but then cried openly and moved gently, as if supplicants, to touch, if not him, then Traveler, his horse. Battle scarred men fell prostrate on the ground and sobbed. Officers astride their still, worn horses wept aloud. Nor were theirs the only tears, for the great man's face glistened as his heart broke and his cause died. He could barely choke out the words—"God bless ole North Carolina."

The formal surrender was set for Monday, the 12th. On Sunday a group of Leander's men came to see him. "Beggin' the Major's pardon, but we'd like a word with you about this here surrender goings on tomorrow."

"What is it, men?"

"Well, we've been figurin'. Now, I reckon we're whupped—sort of—and if we got to stack arms, that's one thing, but, Major, I'll be damned if we're goin' give 'em this flag." The men accompanying their spokesmen stepped forward and unfurled the 16th regimental flag. A profound stillness settled over all those assembled as they looked at the torn, bloody, dirty emblem they had so often followed, so often picked up, so often revered. They remembered the battles, the desperate fighting, and all those who had died under its colors. As if responding to their outpourings, the flag itself lifted, rippled, and rested, the grime and blood and hopes of a nation falling from its frayed edges. "They can have our guns, Major, but they can't take our cause. They can take our bullets, but not our beliefs."

With that the grizzled veteran removed his tattered shirt, took the flag from its staff, and wrapped it around his white, emaciated frame. He put his shirt back on and looked at Leander with tears in his eyes. Barely able to control his emotions himself, Leander said simply, "Dismissed," thereby giving the act his imprimatur.

When the 16th was formed, lo those many years ago, its numbers stood at some 1,300 men. 800 had died since, and 83 were to be paroled at Appomattox; the rest just went off.

Chapter 52

Leander had hoped to ride Horse to the surrender ceremony, but the gaunt, sickly animal could not even support his lifelong rider's diminished weight and collapsed under the effort. Despite his pleadings, Leander was unable to coax his old companion to stand. Othello and Traylor joined him and they all looked on as Horse struggled to breathe.

"Othello, I thought I understood what you felt like when Mule died in harness last week, but I didn't. Unless they're yours, nobody understands. I hate to feel like this when so many men have died so unceremoniously, but the animals—they're innocent of all this. We've worked 'um to death with scant provisions and tainted water. Of course," he sighed, "if men cannot eat, how can animals? But still—"

His comrade's lack of response was tantamount to agreement, but what could be done?

Another casualty lay at their feet. Traylor spoke, "Would you like me to take care of him?"

"If you don't mind, my friend. I don't think I could do it."

"Then go now. It'll be alright."

As Othello and Leander slowly make their way back to their encampment, Leander stared at the ground but addressed Othello. "What then does it mean when I can kill a man but not bring myself to put an animal out of its misery?"

"It means, I think, that you have some humanity left." The two looked at each other for a moment, then continued their desultory walk.

Meanwhile, Traylor lowered his massive frame to the ground and sat beside Horse. He lifted the scarred and worn head onto his lap.

"Horse, you've been a good horse. You've done everything asked of you, never wavered in battle, and have endured where lesser animals failed. It's time to go now. Your race has been run. Perhaps it's best you don't see the surrender anyway, for your old heart would surely break then."

Traylor unfolded his pocketknife and expertly inserted the razor sharp blade into the neck. Horse did not flinch, for to have done so would not become him in the midst of this requiem. As he continued to stroke the now-fevered head and speak his soothing words, the gentle giant enlarged the puncture until a copious flow of blood stained the ground around them, slowly and almost imperceptibly enveloping man and beast in an ochre tapestry. Horse looked up at Traylor, blinked once, and exhaled. It was a breath that seemed to carry with it all past travails. He then closed his eyes, nestled closer, and… died.

It was as it should be.

On the day of reckoning, the Confederate forces formed behind General John B. Gordon. Their decimated ranks held cadaverous men whose uniforms were mere rags, their feet bare, but their lines were straight, their heads erect. The horses were gaunt, bones held together by hide, but they seemed to hold a proud air themselves. They marched past the receiving Federal officer, General Joshua Chamberlain. As they passed, Chamberlain, in a gesture that was at once magnanimous and significant for all time to come, ordered his troops to 'carry arms.' After a moment's hesitation, the men in blue held their muskets to their chests, a quiet salute, a sign of respect understood by all soldiers. When Gordon saw what had occurred, he drew sword, turned his horse, reining it on hindquarters into the air. He then lowered his sword until the tip touched the toe of his boot, a soldier's response. It was over.

Chapter 53

It was over.

Four years. How many men? Hundreds of thousands. A half million? Probably. For what? Leander did not believe that things happened without design. This cataclysm occurred for a purpose. Perhaps it was beyond his time to see it. Now, he just stared, trance-like, into the fire and thought of Thomas and God and family and the South.

Then, that kernel, which must be a particle of divine origin, which exists in all men—yes maybe that was part of it, to assert the divinity in all men—began to blossom, and Leander saw Summer and all the things and people that spoke of tomorrow, and his heart rejoiced in the prospect of living and going on from this place.

Chapter 54

Colonel Stowe had sent word for Leander to report to his campsite as soon as was feasible. Feasible still meant now to the Major, and he did so.

"Leander, I have a General Order from Lee to read to the men. Please gather all that remain in the clearing at five this afternoon."

"Yes, sir."

"Thank you, Major, but I don't think we need to stand on formality any longer."

"Bill, it ain't formality, it's just right."

William smiled at his friend and subordinate, understanding that he spoke from that last vestige which bound them as soldiers, a common thread running through the ages, uniting all warriors. Drawing himself to attention he addressed Leander, "Very well, Major, carry on."

"Yes, sir." Leander turned crisply and left to inform the men.

As the hour drew near, men began to gather at the clearing, which marked the center of their encampment. They arrived in various groupings and in moods that ran the gamut from profound sadness to quiet thanks. None could escape the knowledge that all those who had died did so for a cause that was lost. A residual shock and air of disbelief hung over them as they convened. To a man, they would have followed Lee to hell and back, and now they wanted to hear what he had to say to them. Stowe did not waste time on preliminaries. He stood before them and began to read:

Hdq Army of Northern Virginia
Appomattox Courthouse
April 10th, 1865

General Orders No. 9
After four years of arduous service, marked by unsurpassed courage and fortitude, the army of Northern Virginia has been compelled to yield to overwhelming numbers and resources. I need not tell the

survivors of so many hard-fought battles, who have remained steadfast to the last, that I have consented to this result from no distrust of them, but feeling that valor and devotion could accomplish nothing that would compensate for the loss that must have attended a continuance of the contest, I determined to avoid the useless sacrifice of those whose past services have endeared them to their countrymen. By the terms of the agreement, officers and men can return to their homes and remain until exchanged. You will take with you the satisfaction that proceeds from the consciousness of duty faithfully performed, and I earnestly pray that a merciful God will extend to you His blessing and protection.

With an unceasing admiration of your constancy and devotion to your country, and a grateful remembrance of your kind and generous consideration for myself, I bid you an affectionate farewell.

R.E. Lee

Again, they wept. For many, it was the last time they would do so. No sadness would ever rise to equal this. They sat or stood in that clearing and reduced forever to fingering a blade of grass or pulling at a frayed sleeve. Others looked to the sky or the horizon, lost in a seam of time. No one glanced at another, for they all knew that everyone grieved in their own way, and whatever that meant, it was okay. They had been cleansed. They had been given absolution. They could and must go on. He had said so.

Chapter 55

The change from what had been to what was now was profound for those men who had lived through it. The realization of an idea was dead. The concept that drew these men from home and family to kill others and die themselves was itself gone—it had been purged. It would take years, generations, to cleanse, but it had begun, a necessary beginning.

More immediate, mundane yet vital concerns manifested themselves. Men who, a short time before, had lived day to day, battle to battle, bullet to bullet, and meal to meal, now looked up and saw the future and were numbed by it.

Othello had first thought to go home, with or without Leander, but they realized the climate attending a lone Negro, free or slave or unknown, would be overtly hostile. So he stuck with Leander, who would go to Summer first and then decide what to do next. Traylor had availed himself of Grant's generous terms and convinced the parolers he owned his big horse. Leander, being an officer, was allowed to keep his mount as well as a sidearm. Traylor merely hid his shotgun, believing it did not fall under the terms of a long rifle anyway, and allowed he too would stick with them a while longer before returning to North Carolina. They all rested and healed and ate along with their animals in a fashion unknown to them for years. A week later, they found and repaired a busted ambulance wagon, hooked their two horses to it, and made for Pennsylvania.

The denuded landscape they traveled over was bereft of most everything except memories. They would pull up at a crossroads or a hill or a town and recognize it as the site of this or that battle. The road was marked for them by the death of comrades. Occasionally they would stop and re-bury partially decomposed corpses that had been hurriedly placed in shallow graves or unearthed by animals. It was time consuming, but it could have been someone they knew, and in one case it certainly was, a private Radcliff, a mere boy of 16 from Haywood County they had joshed about having red hair. A letter he had written his grandmother was still in his pocket. Leander took it with him, vowing to place it in the old woman's hands personally. It was a melancholy and surreal odyssey which, unknown to its participants, served a cathartic purpose, and in that manner, healed many wounds, both acknowledged and unspoken.

Chapter 56

The patchwork wagon wobbled over the rise and creaked to a halt. Leander felt a twinge as he gazed at the charred chimneys standing sentinel. So much destruction, so much death. His spirits lifted, however, as he spotted Summer in the loft door, shielding her eyes with both hands as she stared out at them. Once they had gotten underway again, he saw her grab a rope and, using a hay bale for counterweight, drop to the ground. She began running towards them as soon as she touched ground. He could not tolerate the pace either and jumped off the wagon, running to meet her. His gait was awkward, swinging one arm, but he didn't care.

"Leander! Leander!"

"Summer, it's me!" He felt silly, but again didn't care.

They met, and Summer leapt onto him, locking her legs onto his torso, kissing his face and tracing its outline with her fingers.

"Oh, God, Leander, hold me."

"I'll do the best I can." She grabbed his arm and began kissing his hand.

"It's good enough, it's good enough."

The wagon had caught up with them and drew alongside. "Summer, this is Othello, of whom you have heard me speak, and this fellow is Traylor Crockett, a good friend and comrade."

"Welcome, you both are welcome. I know of no higher praise than for Leander to call you his friends. He's told me so much about you. And Mr. Crockett, I have, of late, been regaled with tales of your exploits."

Traylor was somewhat confused.

"Lawd, Lawd! Look at dem skinny white mens. Puny things 'bout to blow away! Couldn't see um' 'tal if dey was to turn sideways." They all looked up to see Sycamore striding towards them like a regent over his domain. Traylor smiled and he, Leander, and Othello let out a simultaneous, "Well, I'll be damned."

"Yes, sir, sorry lookin' riff-raff come up out da South." Laughter and handshakes were exchanged as Traylor inquired of Sycamore how he came to be here. Sycamore puffed up and explained.

"Well, Boss, I comes to dis place 'cause love done drug me. I has took up wid Miss Rose, and my babies gots a momma, too." Sycamore beamed from ear to ear as he snapped the gallowses on his overalls.

"Sycamore Pin Oak! You big dufus, gets back in dis barn and finish your chores. I is da greetin' member of dis family." Rose waddled out to the wagon, wiping her hands on an apron. "Mr. Leander, sho' is good to see you again. Maybe now Miss Summer can quit frettin.'" Sizing up Traylor, Rose observed, "Lawd! Lawd! Look at dis one, big as my Sycamore, just a different shade. And dis must be Othello, da smart one. Well, ya'll come in, we'll see to supper. Come'on, don't dawdle!"

Everyone followed their instructions and moved towards the barn, Sycamore compliantly behind Rose, Leander with his good arm around Summer's waist, while Traylor and Othello brought up the rear leading the horses. As the entourage made its way to their makeshift living quarters, Sycamore could not contain himself any longer and looked over his shoulder at Leander. He winked and announced, "She crazy 'bout me, Boss." Everyone smiled, even Rose, but she soon regained her station and issued her own pronouncement, "You half right, Big un', I is crazy, crazy to take up wid the likes of you. Now come on." Still, the smile played across her brown cherubic face.

Like many houses of its type and era, Bent Oak had its kitchen separate from the main dwelling and attached by a dogtrot. This, combined with the fact that it had been faced with brick, served to save it from the conflagration set by Small. Here then activity reached a fevered pitch as preparations were made and added to for the evening's meal. Around 8, everyone gathered at the big table centered in the barn's cavernous interior. Mary had made sure to seat Sycamore's daughter, Mariposa, next to Othello, although such subterfuge would hardly have been necessary. The two had been smitten with each other from the outset, and their fawning was the source of much amusement. Summer, in a gesture that spoke of strength rather than deference, seated Leander at the head of the table and asked him to return thanks. Somewhat taken aback by the unexpected request, he rose to his feet and looked around the table at these people who had come to mean so much to him. He said, "Let us pray," and bowed his head. The others followed suit. "God, our Father, we come to you with thanks that this war is over. We rejoice in those here and pray for your mercy for those who are not. Lead us in thy light and thy way. Bless this bounty to our bodies and your glory. Amen." A chorus of amen's followed by those seated.

Rose began the procession of platters by offering one of pork chops to Leander, thereby tacitly acknowledging and endorsing Summer's implied transfer of authority. Sweet potatoes, roasting ears, collards, green beans with ham hock, and corn bread made their rounds. A large crock of sweet tea helped wash the feast down, followed by blackberry cobbler. When finished, they all reveled in that mild stupor which follows a good meal.

The laughter and conversation continued under lantern light, until Sycamore, responding to a nudge from Rose, announced for all to gather their sacks in order to set out on a frog-gigging expedition. Naively, Leander scooted his chair back in preparation for leaving when Summer rested a hand on his wrist. He looked to her and saw first how truly beautiful she was in the soft yellow orb glowing around their table. When she barely but perceptively shook her head, he knew the activities were planned for them but did not include them. After everyone left, Summer led Leander up a ramp to a rear portion of the loft that had been sectioned off as her bedroom. There, she methodically undressed him and then gently bathed his hard but ravaged body from a basin. She removed her clothes as Leander audibly gasped. They lay together talking and touching until the ache became intolerable and Summer rolled astride Leander. He was not accomplished at this, but he was willing to learn. He marveled as Summer reached orgasm, thinking he had hurt her. After he was spent, he mistakenly thought they were through until Summer began the riotous, sensual dance all over again. Leander allowed as how this beat killin' and fightin' hands down.

"What news of your uncle?"

"We receive word that he died as a POW in some place called Andersonville."

"I'm so sorry. To think that my people had a hand in the death of someone close to you saddens me beyond words."

"Enough of death and sadness. I love you."

"And I, Summer Will, love you. Thank you."

Hours after their departure, the hunting party returned, making enough noise to warn the next county of their arrival. Leander and Summer had been basking in the afterglow of their lovemaking, caught up in and savoring the moment. They listened as the group drew closer and broke into yet another peal of laughter as Rose chastised Sycamore for yet another transgression, real or imagined. Leander, too, guffawed as he heard Sycamore once again proclaim, "She crazy 'bout me, Boss."

He nuzzled Summer's ear. "How wonderful to hear laughter unadulterated by war."

"Speaking of 'adulterated,' we've got to make an honest woman out of me, don't you think?"

"Yes, yes I do. How do you think we should go about it?"

"Well, we'll send for the Reverend Thomas Strader. He should be able to come in a few days."

"Good, good." Leander fell silent, lost in the light flickering off the massive rafters above them. "And speaking of Thomas, I need to tell you something."

Summer sensing the import of this, rose on an elbow and looked down at Leander. "What is it?"

A biblical injunction stuck in Leander's throat, and he began to weep.

"Leander, what is it? Tell me."

"I killed my brother."

Summer fell back, taking Leander's hand in hers and began searching those same rafters for a response. "Tell me what happened."

Leander did not know how long he spoke, only that when he finished, he had done something necessary.

Summer lay still, never letting go of his hand. "I do not know how to respond to so sad a thing, but I know you, and I know you did what you thought you had to do. That was a place no man should have to visit and a decision no man should have to make. I love you." Leander rolled over, their hands still clasped, her arm encircling his body. In that manner, he slept through the night, untroubled by dreams for the first time since Thomas's death.

Chapter 57

Although Leander was becoming more and more proficient at dressing himself, Summer lent a hand so they would not miss Rose's legendary breakfast fare. The glowing couple walked down the ramp to the embarrassing applause of their friends already seated at the table.

"'Nuff of dat foolishness," Rose proclaimed, silencing the group.

Taking their places from the night before, Leander and Summer then watched in amazement as Sycamore and Traylor devoured plate after plate of ham, grits, fried potatoes, biscuits and red-eye gravy, scrambled eggs, tomatoes, and flapjacks smothered in sorghum. Equally astonishing was the fact they washed it all down with pitcher after pitcher of sweet milk followed by pots of coffee.

The next few weeks rolled on in a joyous stream of what regular folks normally do. With everyone pitching in, the farm began to take on some of its previous luster. Crops were harvested, debris hauled off, and plans for the future were formulated singly and in pairs, together and privately. No waking moment seemed to go by that Othello and Mariposa did not spend it together if possible. They were inseparable and obviously very much in love. The preacher arrived one Thursday morning. Although they had been expecting him, the fact that he was actually there put several folks in a tizzy. Othello, wishing to seize the moment, asked and received permission from Sycamore for Mariposa's hand. Rose told the beaming father of the bride that he was going to make an honest woman out of her, too, and that was the end of that. And so, three couples lined up in the center of the barn, attended by friends, children, and comrades as well as various animals that brayed, mooed, honked or cackled their approval. Following the ceremony, everyone had dinner together, and then the preacher went on to a nearby christening. Darkness set in, and all the joyous newlyweds retired to their marriage beds.

Chapter 58

After their evening meal a few nights later, Leander looked to Summer, who addressed the group. "We need to talk about what's to come. This country will be in a state of upheaval, and in the South, near chaos. We need to decide what is best for us and for our families. Leander and I will be going to his home so he can see his folks and I can meet them. Then, we've decided to come back and make a go of it here. We plan to rebuild the house, and any who wish to stay, may." Traylor vowed to go with them—he missed his mountains and would stay there. Othello said he and Mariposa would return to North Carolina, visit, and then also come back. Summer swore she would never have another home consumed by flames, and therefore the new dwelling would not be constructed like the old one. She had made arrangements with a local brickyard, and Zeke, along with Sycamore, would oversee the delivery of those as well as some foundation stones from an upstate quarry. It was Summer's fervent wish that once the estate was up and running, it would enable them to spend substantial time in both Pennsylvania and North Carolina. She expressed the additional desire to have those down South come spend time with them all there.

Thus the time for departure arrived, and the five of them set out for the Blue Ridge. Two wagons filled with provisions pulled by four horses, trailing one mule, a milch cow, several turkeys, two dogs, a healthy degree of wariness and a great deal of anticipation.

As a surprise, Sycamore, Traylor, and Othello had rigged up a contraption enabling Leander to drive the wagon. They ran both sets of reins across a high yolk, then pinned the left one to his shortened jacket sleeve. With a little practice, he was able to move the team in concert by raising his stump and flicking the right hand. They knew the importance of his being able to do this simple task.

Chapter 59

The trail-weary entourage turned up the rutted, overgrown path into Radcliff Cove following directions from a blacksmith in Waynesville who had repaired their wagon. With the light failing, they made to set up camp, vowing to find the grandmother addressed in the letter Leander carried on the morrow. A broken axle that morning with its attendant and necessary improvisations, in concert with a heavy spell of pushing and pulling, served to make their exhaustion so complete that a fire and some jerky constituted the whole of their activities that evening as they all fell to an early and deep slumber.

The next day broke fair and cool. Two guineas, stupidly intent on pursuing some fleeing grasshoppers, literally walked into camp, thereby offering themselves up for breakfast. A dodger of cornbread and crock of cold buttermilk purchased the previous day completed the morning's fare.

The roadbed had deteriorated to such an extent that Leander decided to unhitch the horses and ride in. Accordingly, he and Traylor set out before eight. They found the hovel an hour later, spotting an old frail woman sitting on its dilapidated porch steps smoking a pipe. Even for these times and place, this was a sty. Leander called out, "Mornin'." Her only acknowledgment was to remove her pipe, spit, and stare. Leander and Traylor rode closer, dismounted and walked to the bottom of the steps, leading their horses. "Are you Jocassee Radcliff's grandmother?"

"I reckon. Who be you?"

"I'm Leander Liner—Captain Liner, and this is Traylor Crockett."

"The boy dead?"

Traylor and Leander looked to each other, shuffled their feet and coughed before Leander spoke. "Yes, I'm sorry, but he is. We brought you a letter." He began to unbutton his shirt pocket with his good hand when a voice bellowed out from within the house.

"Old woman! Bring me a piss pot!"

As she struggled to find purchase on the rickety steps, the bent wisp of a woman offered up an explanation. "That's my nephew. He's poorly." As she turned to remove her cane from its nail on a post, her "poorly" nephew swept the sheet aside which hung limp and dirty across the doorway, ostensibly serving as a screen to ward off the innumerable flies hovering round the detritus flung throughout the yard.

Leander's first thought when he saw the nephew was an alliteration: "fat, filthy and fully growed." He and Traylor exchanged glances and acknowledged agreement as to what was transpiring.

The pallid, obese man-child thrust a chamber pot, sloshing over with excrement, into his aunt's hands and commanded her to empty it as he strode to the porch end to relieve himself. Never once in this undertaking did he concede Leander or Traylor's presence. Leander fished the letter out and handed it to the old woman. "I'm obliged," she said, "but ne're one of us can read. I'm fair at ciphering, but that's all."

Leander looked over the trash-infested yard until he spotted a bench under a willow tree around back. "Let's go sit yonder and I'll be happy to read it to you."

"I'm obliged."

The unlikely couple made their way off after Leander and Traylor exchanged another glance. Once they were out of sight, Traylor tied his mount to a porch rail, wary of allowing it to graze in this dump. He mounted the forgiving steps, walked down the porch, and waited behind while the nephew finished his business. Without turning, the nephew blubbered, "I'm poorly now, leave me be."

"Poorly hell, you're gonna be broke when I finish with you." Having completed the preamble to his task, Traylor kicked the sobbing lout in the ass, sending him flying off the porch. He jumped down astride the man, drawing his long knife. "Git up! Git up or I'll gut you where you lay!"

The man scrambled to his feet, displaying an agility long dormant in such a poor creature. Traylor pinned him against the side of the house, holding his knife to his throat, drawing blood from several places. "Listen to me and listen for all time. Things just changed around here. You ain't 'poorly' no more. You will help that old woman and work and provide for her. We have friends here, and they'll check on her. If I have to come back, you will wish to God I'd killed you now."

"I will! I will!"

"Yes, you will, and you will now. Clean up this mess, fetch some wood, dig a latrine, plow some ground, plant something, do *something!* God, I hate sloth!" The scared, obedient nephew scurried to comply, not knowing which task to begin first but decided on a wheelbarrow to collect trash.

Leander and the old woman settled themselves on the bench. He unfolded the paper with his good hand in preparation for reading its contents. The old woman stopped him, asking first if she might just hold the page for a moment.

"Of course," Leander said, handing it to her. She caressed the paper between her leathery hands, rubbing the creases out in a manner Leander thought must be very much like she had employed when stroking her grandson's red head. Satisfied now that she had touched one of the last things her grandson had held and believing she had extracted the memory and feelings left there, she handed the page back to Leander.

He read:

> *Dear Gammaw,*
> *I love you and want to get that out afore I die. Another fella is putting this down for me. It seems qwar that I have so much to say but when the time comes hit wont come out. Well I reckon I got what matters most in that first part. Hit dont pain none I just feel cold and that is odd to cause hit sure is hot. Well, I rekon this is it. In the sweet by and by, we shall meet on that bewtiful shore. Tell Virgil to pich in and help you.*
> *Your loving grandson,*
> *Private Jocassee Radcliff*

Leander unfolded the paper and gave it to the gray, withered matriarch. "He was a good boy," she said.

"I hope and do truly believe things will be different around here for you from now on."

"Can't say as how I share your faith. Virgil is poorly and I can't fend for myself."

"My friend gave Virgil some medicine. I think he'll be much improved. You'll see."

"Thank you, my friend." The old woman looked off into the distance, her eyes moist with the past. "This war took it out of us, didn't it?"

"That it did, that it surely did."

"Godspeed, son."

"And may he abide with you."

They walked back to the front of the house where Traylor held the horses and Virgil scampered back and forth with his wheelbarrow, collecting trash.

"Well, praise be!" the old woman said. "That must be some powerful medicine you got!"

Traylor smiled as he handed Leander his reins. "Yes, it cuts right through most complaints." They mounted, turned, and rode off, stopping briefly to check on Virgil's welfare.

Chapter 60

Twenty-seven days later, the group camped atop Hogback Mountain, looking down on the valley where Leander, Othello, and Thomas had grown up. The following morning, they broke camp before daylight and made for Rebecca and Levi's house, only a few hours distant. As they rounded a knob on the worn roadway, Leander drew up the team, stopping the lead wagon. Spread out before them were ancient mountains folded into the earth as far as the eye could see, cloaked in a dozen subtle hues of purple, indigo, and blue. The sky held only a few clouds, but what it lacked in number, it made up for in size. As they gazed rapturously at the majesty before them, the rising sun struck the cloud faces, burnishing them like beaten copper from heaven's forge. As it climbed still higher, light contrasted the deep verdant green of nearby mountains with the luminous pearly fog resting quietly between their forested slopes. Summer drew her hand to her mouth as if to catch her exclamation. "Oh, Leander, it is so beautiful." Her eyes traced the serpentine road as it descended and then disappeared, swallowed by the mist. "It's as if we were about to launch into a river… a white river."

Leander inhaled deeply, letting his soul drink. He lifted and then softly dropped the reins like a ripple of leather across the horse's flanks, urging them gently into that eternal stream.

The End

Journal of John Turpin, Captain Company C, 62nd North Carolina Infantry

Sept. 9, 1863 Having been captured this date at Cumberland Gap. It is my intention to write down here the ensuing events and my experiences in hopes that by so doing my family may have a record of this portion of my life. I respectfully request that, if I am unable to do so, these papers be forwarded to my wife, Blaun, in Haywood County, North Carolina. Our surrender to the federal forces here has a strong smell of capitulation. It is not for me to judge how these events came about, but any future inquiry will certainly have my voice added. We were not beaten, now overwhelmed, nor driven back or flanked. The event should have been more vigorously contested. It leaves a very bad taste in my mouth, as it does many others I have spoken with. Indeed, I may have violated protocol in advising some of my men to escape in order to fight another day. Well, military protocol be damned, the requirements of simple manhood dictated otherwise. Be that as it may, after hearing of our surrender, I was soon surrounded by federal cavalry who inquired of me, "Do you surrender?" "Not to a private," I responded.

They then asked if I was an officer. "I am," I replied. It was then that a colonel of what I believe was the 100th Ohio came up and asked again if I surrendered. I said, "As I have no discretion in the matter, I do." The Colonel was very polite and assured me of kind treatment. He turned me over to a subordinate and left. That night, I was removed several miles to the rear along with several of my fellow officers. The night was bitter cold, but I must say we were treated with every kindness by our captors, who offered us whiskey, which helped stave off chills. We were quartered in an open field with no fires.

The next morning, a young Lt. from Wisconsin gave me my first coffee in months and a substantial breakfast. For this I was exceedingly glad. Then we were formed up, counted, and marched off in the direction of some railhead. This took us several days, and it was during this time that I was taken ill with fevers and the runs from I think some raw meat we ate. I cannot find the words for those who attended me in the subsequent days. It was an onerous and thankless task and I have no doubt I would have expired without their ministrations. I awoke one cold bright morning to find myself in Sandusky, Ohio, and could see from the depot the island that was to be our home. Although facing life as a POW for an indefinite time, I was at least free of the confines of sickness. Such is the relative nature of imprisonment. We were loaded aboard a little steamer and taken out. The commander, a Colonel Pierson, met us. Roll was called, and as each answered, we walked up to a window and gave up any cash we had. Upon assuring the clerk we possessed no firearms, those of us with no blankets were given one. Then we were let in with some 2,500 other men. I have run out of paper and ink.

2/14/64 I have accumulated over the last 4 months sufficient monies to obtain paper and ink and will resume this journal. This island is some 2 miles from shore, about 1 mile long, and ½ that in width. The prison itself is an enclosure of ¼ mile square. A high plank surrounds it. On the outer side, a catwalk runs all around, and on this, sentinels are posted day and night. Blockhouses are situated at the two lake facing corners and the entrance. Inside are 13 buildings or houses, each 2 stories high. One of these serves as a hospital. I am given to understand that Johnson's Island is somewhat unique in that it was planned as a POW camp from the beginning and houses only officers. The room I am in is 25 x 35 feet and houses 54 men. We have a stove and burn green wood. Night and day, we wear our blankets to protect us from the cold. As I write the lake is one vast sheet of ice as far as the eye can see and of unbelievable thickness. All in all a unique vista for a southern boy. Those of who have canteens use them double duty for pillows at night and frequently awake to find the water contained therein frozen. Roll call is every morning. We have two details each day, one to police up outside and dispose of waste, another to sweep rooms, cut, split, and haul wood. Rations are good and issued every Sunday. The bread is baked here on the island and is excellent, but we are only given one loaf for 4 men. We have access to a sutler for such things as tobacco, stationary, and stamps. Packages from home are faithfully delivered after being examined for contraband. We have a post office of sorts where letters are received and sent.

2/19/64 400 Prisoners sent out. We believe to Point Lookout, Maryland, but not for exchange, we think, because they were chosen alphabetically.

2/23/64 Previous week's weather so cold I could not write. Ink froze in pen.

Tried to sleep under 6 blankets but could not, too cold even with a bunkmate. Yesterday was anniversary of Washington's birth. Federals had mock celebration. We had our own with many eloquent speeches by our men.

2/25/64 On occasion one of our men will attempt escape. Once in a while, one will make it. This can only be done when the lake is frozen over. Because we have such bad water on the island, we are permitted to go to the lake every day. Last week, one of our enterprising fellows got hold of a Yankee overcoat and made off.

3/1/64 I have not addressed my state of mind here, but will do so briefly, for that is all I can manage. Yes, we are, all of us, despondent. Day after day, away from all we hold dear, not knowing how our families fare, wondering how our comrades are doing. The filth and vulgarity grow each day. We live in constant hope that a successful spring campaign will afford us exchange opportunities.

3/5/64 A day of sunshine and the men turn out of their holes like bees in spring.

3/6/64 Snow again and cold.

3/8/64 Northern clergymen come in and offer their services. We should have known better. They do not wish to preach the gospel but lecture us on abolition.

3/12/64 Favoritism in exchanges riles us. Men who have been here 12 months are kept while others imprisoned only 3 are subjects of special exchange.

3/14/64 I have received several letters from my men housed at Point Lookout. They are well. I now have enough bedclothes to sleep alone.

3/15/64 Again, I think we are unique in that we are now allowed to write to relatives only. This has prompted an enormous increase in cousins and aunts.

4/10/64 Nothing to write, the blues have settled over me. No exchanges.

4/11/64 Went to see the theatre group formed by prisoners today. Had my first good laugh in weeks.

4/15/64 We understand Grant is now in command and has crossed the Rapidan. Our captors tell us daily of his exploits. We do not know what to believe.

4/16/64 I look with trepidation and hope upon the return of warm weather. The sun will be welcome but the stench will be awful.

4/17/64 Sedgewick's Corp has been called to the front. We are now guarded by state militia. They are cold and cruel men. Is it not ironic that those who have actually experienced battle treat those whom they have captured with more kindness than those who have set out the war at home?

4/18/64 The accounts given us by the guards mean Grant has killed 100,000 more men than Lee has and has driven the army of Northern Virginia into the Gulf of Mexico.

4/19/64 I have a small number of wildflowers gleaned from our cemetery. The care and attention I devote to them is all out of proportion, yet they transport me to another time, another place.

5/23/64 I believe each side now houses 60,000-70,000 prisoners, but still the Federals will not exchange. I think they know our men will return to the field, theirs will not.

6/2/64 Two escape tunnels, one from a blockhouse, one from the dead house, were discovered. I think we have spies among us.

6/3/64 Cold still. Stoves taken away. No glass in windows. Filth everywhere.

6/4/64 A new rule. Any escape attempt means all will be punished with no rations.

6/5/64 One old man put it succinctly this morning at roll call as he shivered: "I don't mind freezing in winter but damned if something ain't wrong with a place where you do it in summer."

6/6/64 Another new rule. No letter can be received that is over ½ page in length. How cruel. Imagine getting a letter from loved ones after a year here, only to be given the envelope and watch the letter burn. Damn these people!

6/7/64 Exchange rate is now 7 cents to 1 dollar. Plug of tobacco is 1 dollar, a pound is 2.50. Butter is 40 cents per pound.

6/25/64 No rain since May. More and more officers arriving even though all those captured from Lee are sent to Maryland and Delaware. This does not look good. We get many prisoners from Sherman's activities.

7/1/64 Despair. We get no news or letters.

8/12/64 Fort Powell surrendered. Federal fleet in Mobile Bay.

8/29/64 Secretary of War forbids anyone sending us anything.

9/1/64 The Chicago Convention will determine our fate. We think McClellan will be nominated.

9/2/64 Rations are practically nonexistent. We have taken to eating the rats. They are fat and gentle and easily killed. 10 or 12 dressed for the pot make a good stew.

9/27/64 We hear that Petersburg and Mobile have surrendered. I fear all is lost. Oh poor, poor South. What now?

10/6/64 I am to be sent to Point Lookout today.

10/10/64 I am to be exchanged tomorrow. I fear our cause is lost, our way unsure.

For those men believed in something.
They counted life a light thing to lay down in the faith they bore.
They were terrible in battle, they were generous in victory.
They rose up from defeat to fight again, and while they lived, they were formidable.
There were not enough of them, that is all.

    `John W. Thompson
    Lieutenant Colonel
    U.S. Marine Corps
    Lone Star Preacher

Afterword

This story is fictional. It is, however, fiction as firmly ensconced in accurate historic and military data as was possible for me to access. With few exceptions, the formation and ensuing battle record of the 16th and 62nd North Carolina Infantry Regiments are taken from official records and remembrances of its soldiers. I have attempted to weave a story from fact and informed conjecture. Leander and Thomas Liner were real people, the latter my great-grandfather, the former his brother. Unlike the story line, both survived the war. In point of fact, Thomas was a member of the 16th, Leander the 25th North Carolina. I have placed them both—eventually—in the same regiment to facilitate the story telling. Captain John Turpin was indeed a Captain with the 62nd North Carolina and my great-great-grandfather. Both Thomas and Turpin were taken prisoner, Liner at Piedmont, Virginia, and Turpin at Cumberland Gap, Tennessee. Subsequently, Thomas was housed at Point Lookout, Maryland, and Captain Turpin on Johnsons Island in Lake Erie. After the war, both walked home and Thomas married Turpin's daughter, Almeda. Leander moved to Texas after the war. The rest of his life is unknown to me.

George Nimrod Rush was one of the first physicians to practice in Macon County. He employed a black midwife to assist him whose name was Mary. I am told their relationship was more than just professional. Indeed, family legend holds that Mary is buried beside him. I hope so. Dr. Rush was my great-great-grandfather.

All these people were my ancestors and I am all these people.

George Gary Roland

BIBLIOGRAPHY

Addey, Markinfield. *Stonewall Jackson: The Life and Military Career of Thomas Jonathan Jackson, Lieutenant-General in the Confederate Army.* New York: Charles T. Evans, 1863

The American Heritage Dictionary of the English Language. 3rd ed. Boston: Houghton Miffin, 1992.

Bartlett, John, comp. *Familiar Quotations.* 12th ed. Boston: Little Brown, 1948.

Blanton, Wyndham Bolling. *Medicine in Virginia in the Nineteenth Century.* Richmond: Garrett and Massie, 1933.

Boatner, Mark M III. *The Civil War Dictionary.* 1988; reprint, New York: Vintage Civil War Library, 1991.

Borke, Heros von. *Memoirs of the Confederate War for Independence*: London (Blackwood) 1866; reprinted, New York, 1938.

Brock, R.A. *The Appomatox Roster.* New York: Antiquarian Press. 1962.

Casdorph, Paul Douglas. *Lee and Jackson: Confederate Chieftains.* New York: Paragon House, 1992.

Clark, Walter. *Histories of the Several Regiments and Battalions from N.C. in the Great War 1861-65.* Vols

Katcher, Philip. The Civil War Source Book. Reprint, New York: Facts on File, 1995.

Cooke, John Esten. *A Life of Gen. Robert E. Lee*. New York: D. Appleton, 1871.

Current, Richard Nelson, ed. *Encyclopedia of the Confederacy*. 4 vols. New York: Simon and Shuster, 1993.

Davis, Burke. *They Called Him Stonewall*. New York, Rinehart, 1954.

Dilorenzo, Thomas. *The Real Lincoln: A New Look at Abraham Lincoln, His Agenda, and an Unnecessary War*. Pittsburg: Three Rivers Press, 2003.

Faust, Drew Gilpin. *The Creation of Confederate Nationalism: Ideology and Identity in the Civil War South*. Baton Rouge: Louisiana State University Press, 1988.

Fishel, Edwin C. *The Mythology of Civil War Intelligence*. Civil War History, 10 (1964).

Freeman, Douglas Southall. *Lee's Lieutenants. A Syudy in Command*. 3 vols. New York: Charles Scribner's Sons, 1942-44.

Mosocco, Ronald. *The Chronological Tracking of the American Civil War Per the Official Records of the War of the Rebellion*. 2nd ed. Williamsburg, VA. James River Publications, 1993.

Robertson, James I. Jr. *Stonewall Jackson: The Man, The Soldier, The Legend*. New York: MacMillan Publishing Co., 1997.

_____. *General A.P. Hill The Story of a Confederate Warrior*. New York: Random House. 1987.

Rowse, A.L. *The Annotated Shakespeare*. New York: Clarkson N. Potter Publisher, 1978.

Sears, Stephen W. *Landscape Turned Red: The Battle of Antietum*. New York: Ticknor and Fields, 1983.

Shaara, Jeff. *The Last Full Measure*. New York: Ballentine Publishing Group, 1998.

Shaara, Michael. *The Killer Angels*: New York: Ballentine Books, 1975.

Sibley, Ray F Jr. *The Confederate Order of Battle. The Army of Northern Virginia*. Vol 1. Shippensburg, Pa.: White Mane Publishing Co., 1996.

Sorrell, Moxley G. *Recollections of a Confederate Staff Officer*. New York, Neale, 1905.

Starke, Richard Bories. *Surgeons and Surgical Care in the Confederate States Army*. Virginia Medical Quarterly, 87 (1986).

Thomas, Emory Morton. *Bold Dragoon: The Life of J.E.B. Stuart*. New York: Harper and Row, 1986.

The Library of Congress. Civil War Desk Reference. Wagner, Margaret, Gary Gallagher and Paul Finkleman. New York: Simon and Shuster, 2002.

Weat, Jeffrey D. *General James Longstreet, The Confederacy's Most Controversial Soldier*: A Biography. New York: Simon and Shuster, 1993.

Printed in the United States
23555LVS00006B/73